I0671167

The Brand of the I.D.B.

by G. H. Teed

Illustrated by Eric Parker

First published in the Union Jack magazine,
Series 2, No. 1016, dated 31 March, 1923.

Stillwoods Edition

Stillwoods.Blogspot.Ca

Catalogue Information:
Title: The Brand of the I.D.B.
Author: G. H. Teed (1881-1938)
Illustrated by: Eric Parker
First published anonymously in the Union Jack magazine, Series 2, No. 1016, dated 31 March, 1923.
This Edition by: Stillwoods, 2021
ISBN Canada: 978-1-989788-66-0
Blog: Stillwoods.Blogspot.Ca
Author Blog: http://ghteed.blogspot.com/
Storefront: http://www.lulu.com/spotlight/lulubook22

Copyright © Doug Frizzle and/or Stillwoods, 2021.
Cover adapted from the original.

Teed Bibliography Link:
https://tinyurl.com/ve25d42s
The link above should go to a spreadsheet of all known Teed stories. The list is annotated with various information on the stories and my progress with recapturing the work.   /drf

The library of Teed's stories increases almost daily. Check at the Storefront link above for the latest arrivals. /drf

Keywords: Sexton Blake, British fictional detective, Tinker, Yvonne Cartier, Africa

Cautionary Note: This series of books by Stillwoods are intended to make the stories of G. H. Teed, born in New Brunswick, Canada, available to collectors and researchers. The editor, or rather digitizer has not intentionally altered the original publication.

This story may contain language and racial terms that are not appropriate to today. I apologize for them; I know that the author was using his voice to excite and entertain an adventurous English audience. These works were published from 82 to 110 years ago. Most every work has characters of redeeming ethnicity within.

I hope you enjoy and share these stories; I have.
Doug Frizzle

The BRAND of the I.D.B.!

A STORY OF SEXTON BLAKE in AFRICA

This is a yarn that will please all U. J. readers—and certainly those who know anything of Africa. Many times lately requests have been received from South African readers for a tale introducing Sexton Blake into their part of the world—and here it is! Written by the U. J.'s. star author, this yarn combines the virile atmosphere of the great out-doors with that captivating touch of first-hand knowledge that travel alone can give. Also, it's a grand study in the detective methods of SEXTON BLAKE, YVONNE, & TINKER.

A Stone Filter   /drf

A story of Sexton Blake in Africa featuring also Mdlle. Yvonne and Tinker.

This is a yarn that will please all U. J. readers —and certainly those who know anything of Africa. Many times lately requests have been received from South African readers for a tale introducing Sexton Blake into their part of the world —and here it is written by the U. J.'s, star author, this yarn combines the virile atmosphere of the great out-doors with that captivating touch of first-hand knowledge that travel alone can give. Also, it's a grand study in the detective methods of SEXTON BLAKE, YVONNE, & TINKER.

PETER, Mademoiselle Yvonne's red-headed office-boy, had just departed whistling, on his way to the post office, and the clatter of his heels on the stairs had scarcely died away when the door of the outer office swung open, and a man entered. He stood hesitatingly by the rail for a moment, and then slowly removed a battered felt hat — which was of the type more appropriate to the far places of the earth rather than London.

Margaret Bryan, Yvonne's private secretary, glanced up from her desk; then she rose and came across to the rail. Miss Bryan was an extremely neat and efficient young woman who had been with Yvonne since the latter had opened her consulting offices in Oxford Street. She had quickly demonstrated her ability, and in the affairs of the office was in Yvonne's complete confidence. Miss Bryan was not particularly young —perhaps thirty or so —but she had a most attractive presence and charming manners which soon won the regard of all who knew her. Her features were fine and regular, and had it not been for the thick-lensed glasses she was forced to wear on account of shortsightedness, she would have been almost beautiful.

In anything touching her private affairs, Margaret Bryan was very reserved. Even Yvonne knew little more than that she lived with her mother in a small flat in West Kensington, and although Yvonne had wondered now and then if romance had ever entered the other girl's life, she had never attempted to force her confidence.

Not until she had almost reached the rail where the stranger stood was she able to see his features distinctly. As her eyes rested on his forehead a faint shudder went through her, but she gave no outward sign of this as she smiled and asked him what he wished.

It was only then that she noticed that the man was staring at her with distended eyes, and that he had backed away from the rail, fumbling with his hat.

It is little wonder that Margaret Bryan had felt a sense of shock when her eyes had first encountered the man's forehead.

It was rare indeed that one so disfigured walked abroad openly, and it was this undoubtedly which had caused the visitor to keep his soft hat pulled well down over his eyes while passing through the streets.

At first glance one would have thought that the skin had been deliberately cicatriced in some mad attempt to cause as much disfigurement as possible. But, on closer examination, one could see that the whole forehead from temple to temple had been pricked out in some sort of crazy tattoo design.

A strange whim for a man to have to thus stamp himself apart from his follows!

Men who wander over the rim of the Great Beyond have strange fancies at times, and it is no uncommon thing to find these fancies expressed in tattooed designs on limbs and body; but on the visible part of the features very, very rarely. And yet even Miss Bryan, for all her shortsightedness, could see that the markings had been boldly done.

For the rest, the man's features were normal.

His eyes were deep sunk and lined at the corners like those of one who has been accustomed to gaze across vast distances of sea or desert. His nose was arched and big; his chin and mouth concealed by a straggly brown beard, ill-kempt.

His clothes, like his hat, were more in keeping with the wide outdoors than with the environs of a great city, for his shirt was of khaki, the collar open, his trousers of the same material, and his coat, a shabby, well-worn shooting-coat padded across the shoulders like those worn by hunters in tropical countries.

It would have been a difficult problem to guess his age correctly. His figure and bearing were those of a man in his early thirties, but his eyes and the sun-marked wrinkles beneath them might have been those of a man of fifty.

Margaret Bryan did not see the strong, brown fingers clutch the rail as he stepped back, staring in wide amaze at her, but her head came up sharply as he cried hoarsely:

"Margaret!"

She laid her hands on the rail and bent forward. Then her fingers clutched the sleeve of his coat, as she whispered:

"You —who are you that you call me that?"

He swept her hand from his arm and laughed harshly.

"Who am I?" he echoed mockingly. "Who am I? Well might you ask! There was a time when you didn't need to ask that question. You knew me well enough then. But it was easy to forget when you wanted to. Who am I? Ask them, on the convicts' breakwater in South Africa who I am and they will tell you. They will remember me longer than you."

"You—lie—when—you—say—I—have—forgotten—"

Slowly, pitifully, in a strangled whisper the words came from between the girl's white lips. Every vestige of blood had drained from her face, and as the last word trailed off into a choking sob, she slumped to the floor in a dead faint.

For a moment the man stared futilely at the crumpled heap on the floor. His eyes lifted and sought first the door leading to the private office, then that which opened on to the hall. He hesitated, as if he would retreat; then muttering something, he tossed his hat aside and vaulted the rail.

Bending down, he picked up the prostrate figure of the girl and carried her across to a wide leather couch which stood against the wall. Then he gazed about frowningly in search of water. In one corner he spied a stone filter.

He seized the glass which stood beside it, and hurried back to the girl. He took out his handkerchief, and, thrusting his arm beneath her head, began dabbing her temples with water.

He was still so engaged when the door of the private office opened and Mademoiselle Yvonne emerged, to stand gazing in stupefaction at the uncouth figure of a strange man employed in trying to bring her usually unemotional secretary out of a fainting spell. Swiftly Yvonne crossed the room and bent down.

"What is it? What has happened?" she asked curtly. "How is it that I find Miss Bryan like this?"

Her eyes turned to the man as she spoke, and although she noticed at once the awful disfigurement of the forehead, Yvonne was too well schooled to give any sign. In that single glance, too, she took in each detail of his appearance, and for a moment she wondered if it had been the shock of his disfigurement that had caused Margaret Bryan to faint. But the next instant Yvonne discarded that, for she knew the girl was too well balanced to succumb to what, after all, was more a thing to rouse pity than repulsion.

"I—I—" stammered the man.

"Leave her to me," interrupted Yvonne crisply. "No; wait a moment."

With that she sprang up and re-entered her private room. She returned a few seconds later, carrying a bottle of smelling salts. Then she pushed the stranger away.

"Stand over there!" she ordered. "Don't attempt to leave the room. I have a few questions to ask you."

The man nodded and obeyed. He stood gazing at them sombrely, while Yvonne applied the smelling salts to the girl's nostrils, petting and soothing her as she did so. At last Margaret's lids fluttered and opened, and she made an effort to sit up.

"Not just yet, dear," said Yvonne. "Wait a few moments."

"I am all right now, mademoiselle," she answered faintly. "I was silly to faint. I —"

Then her eyes encountered the man, and she pressed closer to Yvonne.

Yvonne's eyes narrowed as she gazed across Margaret's head towards the stranger. She needed nothing more than that clutch of Margaret's to tell her that in some way this strange visitor had been the cause of the girl's collapse. But she was greatly puzzled to account for it.

If the man had entered the office with a menace of some sort, then, when Margaret fainted, it was odd that he should have tried to bring her round. It would have seemed more natural if he had cleared out as quickly as possible.

But he had obeyed Yvonne readily, and seemed not to be contemplating escape.

And yet, as soon as Margaret had looked at him, she had trembled and pressed tighter against Yvonne's arm, as if for protection.

"Do you care to tell me what happened?" asked Yvonne gently. "Has this man frightened you?"

"Perhaps it would be simpler if I told you what happened," broke in the stranger. "Miss Bryan and I knew each other some years ago. I had no idea when I came here this morning that I should find her here. She was equally surprised at my appearance, although she didn't recognise in me the man she had known before. Nor is it any wonder," he added bitterly, "that is all, and I think Miss Bryan will soon recover"— the latter remark with a sarcastic twist of the lips.

"I am not interested in what you think," rejoined Yvonne coldly. "I am only interested in why I find my friend and secretary in this condition."

"Your secretary!" he exclaimed. "Are you Mademoiselle Cartier?"

"Yes, I am she."

"Well, it was you I came to see."

"You came to see me? Why?"

"Well, I guess it doesn't matter now. I didn't know I should find her" —and he made a gesture towards Margaret— "here; and, besides, I thought you were different."

Yvonne held up her hand.

"Wait," she said. Then she turned back to Margaret. "Do you care to tell me more?" she asked. "Don't do so if you would rather not, dear; but I am worried about you."

Miss Bryan sat up and fixed her eyes on the man. She had now regained control of herself, and only a slight tremor in her tones told that she was still fighting down the emotion that had seized upon her.

"Are you Jim Bridger?" she asked in a low tone.

The man bowed ironically.

"Fancy that!" he exclaimed. "She recognises me at last!"

"That is enough of that!" snapped Yvonne, getting to her feet. "You have upset this girl sufficiently already. Use a different tone in this office."

His eyes narrowed, and he bent forward slightly from the hips.

"A different tone!" he cried. "Oh. I'll use a different tone all right! Any tone will do for a woman who deserts a man when trouble overtakes him. It's easy, I dare say, for you to stand there and tell me to use a different tone. But try a few years on the Breakwater in South Africa, and see what tone you learn to use there!

"Stand up and take the I.D.B. (Illicit Diamond Buyer) brand on your forehead, so that all the world will know that you have been a felon, and see what sort of a tone you learn with that!

"Bah! I have been a fool. I came here because I was told that you could help a man. I might have known it would be like this, but I didn't think I would hit a bunch of hysterical women, and one of them as disloyal as a—"

"Stop!"

Margaret Bryan had risen to her feet, and was standing facing the man, both hands pressed against her heart.

"You lie —you lie —you lie!" she cried furiously, and Yvonne gazed in dumbfounded amazement at the sudden outburst on the part of one whom she had never dreamed could be swept by such a wild passion. "I was never disloyal in thought or word or deed. It was you,

5

and you know it!"

The man started forward, his eyes fixed on her in disbelief. Yvonne had drawn a little to one side. She had determined to let them talk until she gathered some idea of what it was about.

"If you were not disloyal, why did you not answer my letter?" he demanded harshly. "In that letter I told you I was in trouble, and I told you I was innocent. But you ignored it completely. You let me go through that trouble without a word. You let me be branded with the cursed brand of the I.D.B. without a word of comfort. You let me go to the Breakwater for ten long years with never a word all that time. And you say you were not disloyal. Bah!"

"Your letter," she whispered. "I never received any letter from you. I swear that is the truth, Jim!"

The man sank back against the rail, his expression that of one who is utterly baffled. But before he could reply Yvonne held up her hand. She had heard the clatter of Peter's boots on the stairs.

"Someone is coming," she said. "Go into my room, Margaret. And you, sir, follow!"

Yvonne was just closing the door when Peter entered. She told him that she was not to be disturbed; then, motioning Margaret to a chair, she seated herself at her desk and lit a cigarette.

"Let him speak, please," answered Margaret in a small voice.

Yvonne turned to the man.

"Are you ready to do so?"

"I am quite ready, but it won't do any good now."

"Never mind about that. I shall judge when I have heard all. You may be seated if you wish."

He muttered something and sank into a chair. Yvonne studied him for a few seconds, then she proffered him the big silver box of cigarettes.

He selected one diffidently, then, when he had lit it, he leant forward and began to talk.

The man with the tattooed forehead was still bending over the girl when the door of the private office opened and Mademoiselle emerged, to stand gazing in stupefaction at the uncouth figure of a stranger trying to bring her unemotional secretary out of a fainting spell. (*Prologue.*)

"I'LL explain first why I came here this morning," he said. "I only arrived from Africa a few days ago, but before I left there I had made up my mind to come and consult you on my arrival. I may as well tell you now that a man whom you helped once suggested it to me."

"Who was that?"

"A man named Simmons —Dave Simmons. He said he got into some trouble one time with your brother, Bob Cartier, and you got them out of it."

Yvonne's eyes grew strained, as the stranger spoke of her brother Bob, for there had been a very deep bond of affection between the sister and brother, and it had been a deep shock to Yvonne when Bob had been killed in the war.

"You knew my brother?" she asked slowly.

"I met him once," answered the stranger. "He was dead square."

He could have said nothing which would have gone to Yvonne's heart more than that.

Bob Cartier had been wild and headstrong. He was a born rover, and was always to be found mixed up in the raw life of some distant frontier. He was continually getting into scrapes, most of them harmless enough, and Yvonne had been as continually engaged in getting him out of them.

But never for a single moment had their affection been impaired, and if he achieved nothing greatly material while he did live, Bob Cartier redeemed all his wild and reckless past in the glorious way he went to his death.

Anyone who had ever known him would always have a claim on her attention.

"I remember the time of which you speak," she said softly, "and I remember Mr. Simmons. Proceed, please."

"Just over ten years ago I went to South Africa," he went on. "I was prospecting round in different districts for some time, and then I joined the diamond rush to Speyfontein. I staked out a claim there, and struck it rich. Then one of the big companies heard about it, and got after it. That always happens in South Africa. The companies have got the diamond game tied up tighter than a drum. The throwing open of new districts for prospecting is nothing but a farce, and no better to-day than it was then.

"But I didn't know about that then. I was green, and I was easily fooled. They framed me, and they got me. It doesn't take long to tell how.

"You know, of course, that every diamond found in South Africa is supposed to be registered. There are plenty that aren't, but they are kept out of sight. The penalty is heavy, and in the old days any man found in possession of an unregistered diamond was arrested as an illicit diamond buyer, and sent to the Breakwater for a term. In those days, too, he was branded on the forehead with the letters "I.D.B.", which marked him for life. It was the finish of a man. Well, I say they framed me.

"There was a sergeant of the Mounted who was on duty in the diamond district where my claim was. I was in Speyfontein one night, seeing about supplies, and trying to pick up a partner to help me work the claim, when this sergeant nabbed me. It was in the bar of an hotel there, and there were plenty of people round. Recollect I had no idea then that the big people had put up a game on me in order to get possession of my claim, for, of course, a convicted man can't file one.

"Now, when I went into that bar I hadn't a diamond of any sort on me. That is the plain truth. But when this sergeant held me and searched me there he found two stones in my pocket. I knew that the only way he could dig up a stone from my pockets was to plant it there while he was making the search.

"That is what he did, but I hadn't the ghost of a chance to prove it. It was evidence enough to settle my fate, and, of course, I was arrested.

"Well, they didn't get me to the Breakwater that time. I was in gaol a long time, and I fought the case every way I could. But they beat me, and I was sentenced to the Breakwater.

"But to go back a little. When I left England I was engaged to be married to a girl. That girl is Margaret Bryan, who sits there before you. When I got into this trouble I wrote to her, telling her all about it, and I gave it to a man who promised to post it for me.

"I saw him afterwards, and he told me he had done so. I waited and waited for a reply, but none came, and then —well, I didn't care what happened.

"They sentenced me, but they didn't get me to the Breakwater — not that time. Sergeant Walters, the same who was in the pay of the big company that had framed me, was to take me down from Speyfontein, but he never got me there. I escaped on the way, and managed to get across into Portuguese East.

"Then I turned I.D.B. in earnest. If I had the name, and had been ruined in getting it, I reckoned I might as well have the game.

"After my escape, Walters had been reduced to the ranks, and you can guess that his one aim was to run me to earth. Well, he wouldn't have done so if I hadn't been betrayed by a man I thought I could trust. Anyway, they got me, and that time I went to the Breakwater."

He paused and brushed his hand across his forehead.

"That was when they branded me, too," he muttered, as if to himself. Then he recovered.

"I served my sentence there," he continued, "and as soon as I was released I went to Beira. In Beira I had my forehead tattooed to cover up the letters that had been branded there, and that is why it is like it is to-day."

He was not looking at Margaret Bryan. If he had been, he would have seen a spasm of pain and compassion cross her face. But Yvonne was looking at the girl, and all the time she was listening to the man she was reading the story which Margaret's eyes were telling.

"I went back into the I.D.B. game again," he said, after a short pause. "I stayed in it just long enough to get a stake together, and to 'get' the man who had betrayed me. I fixed him all right, and he is now down on the Breakwater where he sent me. But the details of that won't interest you.

"My chief aim, however, was to find out exactly how I had been framed by the big company. I wanted to find the man who had been behind it, and to make him pay —pay with interest, what he had made me endure.

"When I had made my stake, I went back, to Speyfontein. Things had changed a good deal there, and there wasn't much risk of my being recognised. I scouted round for some time, and at last struck a line I thought was worth while following up. I got on to that through the man who had been the only friend to me during the first trial."

"Do you mean the man to whom you gave the letter to post to Mar —to Miss Bryan?"

"Yes, He couldn't tell me much, but he did tell me that it was pretty well known that I had been "framed" by a man of the name of

Harrison —one Mike Harrison. Since then he has grown wealthy, and is now Sir Michael, I understand."

"Why, yes —if it is the same. There is a Sir Michael Harrison here in London. I believe he is heavily interested in South African gold and diamond mines;"

"That will be the same," said the man grimly. "Well, I found I couldn't do anything much in Speyfontein. He has a son in charge of things out there; but it was the old man I was after. So I started for England. In Durban I ran into Dave Simmons, and it was his suggestion that I look you up as soon as I got here. He said you might be able to suggest something.

"That is why I was here this morning. I didn't expect to find Mar —Miss Bryan here. And now I will go."

He made as if to rise, but Yvonne held up her hand.

"What did you say your name was?"

"I didn't say, but it is Bridger —Jim Bridger."

"Very well, Mr. Bridger —just wait a moment." Then Yvonne turned to Margaret. "Did you receive no letter from Mr. Bridger, Magaret?"

"No; I received nothing after the last letter which came, and that said nothing about any diamond strike, or any trouble, I heard nothing more, although I wrote for six months longer. I —I never knew what had happened until a man came to see me. He said that he had been with Jim —Mr. Bridger —in South Africa, and that he had asked him to tell me that he —that he had married a girl out there."

"What!" Jim Bridger fairly yelled the exclamation at the girl's bent head, but she paid no attention. She was weeping now, and Yvonne could see that she was near the breaking-point. She signed for Bridger to say nothing more to Margaret just then.

"There seems to have been a very serious misunderstanding," she said quietly —"an understanding that has victimised you both. It will need clearing up. But, first, there are several things to consider."

She rose as she spoke, and crossed to Margaret. She laid her arm across the girl's heaving shoulders, and said gently:

"Tell me, dear, can you describe this man who brought you that message?"

"It was a long time ago." sobbed Margaret.

"He —he was a short, stout man, very dark, and I —I think he limped."

Yvonne turned her head as Jim Bridger came to his feet.

"Tell me," he cried, "did he have a long scar over one eye —the left?"

"Y-yes."

"Do you recognise the description?" asked Yvonne quickly.

"Recognise it? Why, that is the description of the man to whom I gave the letter to post."

"Ah! Do you happen to know if he came to England about that time?"

"Why —why, now that I think of it, he went off somewhere, but I never heard where he went."

"Then it never occurred to you that he might have been in the pay of the man who was behind the whole thing?"

Jim Bridger shook his head in bewilderment.

"No —never occurred to me," he muttered.

"Mr. Bridger, I want you to go into the other room for a few minutes. Don't leave; I want to talk to you again."

He nodded, and made for the door. As he passed Margaret, he hesitated, but then went on. As soon as the door had closed, Yvonne bent close to the girl.

"Margaret, dear," she said softly, "I have no wish to pry into your secrets, but I want you to tell me one thing if you will."

"I will, mademoiselle," answered the girl. "You have been so kind to me, you have the right to ask me anything."

"Then tell me, Margaret, do you still love Jim Bridger?"

"I —I —Oh, yes! There has never been anyone else. I —I thought he had forgotten me. It broke my heart; I didn't want to live —I didn't know what to do. But I had my mother, and I had to go on year after year and try to forget. Oh. I can't say any more!"

"It isn't necessary, dear. You have told me what I wanted to know. Now, I want you to wait here for a few minutes. I shall be back soon."

With that Yvonne rose and opened the door to the outer office. Jim Bridger was seated on the couch, gazing moodily at the floor, while Peter was casting surreptitious glances towards the strange figure, and, if the truth were told, building all sorts of hectic theories to account for the tattoo-marks on the forehead.

He had just come to the conclusion that the man must have been seized by Chinese pirates off the coast of China at some time and sold into slavery, where he had been branded, and, after wild and terrible dangers, had managed to escape, when Yvonne cut his romancing short by saying:

"Peter, I want you to go round to Baker Street. Give my compliments to Mr. Blake, and say that I should be pleased if he and Tinker will dine with me this evening."

"Y-yes, miss."

Peter jumped up and reached for his cap. He might be interested in the stranger, but that interest soon vanished at the prospect of going round to Baker Street, for nothing was quite so big in Peter's life — except his admiration for Yvonne—than his awe of the famous Sexton Blake and his envy of Tinker, especially when the latter unbent enough to acknowledge Peter's existence.

Therefore, it was not long before the clatter of his heels could be heard as he dashed down the stairs. Then Yvonne stood in front of Bridger looking very slim and sweetly serious as she gazed down at him.

"Mr. Bridger," she said abruptly, "have you told me the whole truth?"

"Every word that I have spoken is the truth," he answered, looking up.

And Yvonne knew that he did not lie.

"When you went out to South Africa., did you love Margaret Bryan?"

"Did I? Why she was everything to me!"

Yvonne nodded her little head wisely, "And supposing you had not believed what you did about her, would you have still continued to love her?"

"Why talk of that?" he asked bitterly. "What is done, is done, and it can't be un done."

"Do you mean you still doubt her word?"

"Oh, what am I to think?" he cried desperately. "Think of what I went through on that cursed Breakwater. Look at me today. I am exactly thirty-four years old and I look fifty. In order to conceal the brand they put on me, I was forced to disfigure myself even worse.

"When, people see my forehead they flinch from me as if I was something unclean. Do you think a man who lives day in and day out with that curse upon him can be expected to reverse his belief in a moment?"

13

"You have suffered —have suffered heavily," said Yvonne gently. "But even that does not give you the right to think that others have not suffered, too. Have you no thought for what Margaret has suffered? Do you think it was easy for her to pick up the threads of her life and carry on bravely, thinking that you had forgotten her, and had married another girl?"

The man muttered something but Yvonne could not make out what he said.

"You men are sometimes very foolish," she said softly. "You are egoists, and at times your egoism blinds you to great truths. Mr. Bridger, I can make a statement here and now which you cannot deny."

"What do you mean?"

"This —you still love Margaret Bryan!"

"I —Well, what if I do? Do you suppose she has any use now for a man with a face marked as mine is marked? Do you think she wants anything to do with a felon?"

Yvonne laid her hands on his shoulders. "Mr. Bridger, I have already said that you men are very foolish at times, and also blind. In the next room is one of the finest girls I have ever known. At this moment she is suffering tortures of uncertainty. I never dreamed that she was carrying such a load of suffering in her life. She has been braver than most women would have been.

"And you say she couldn't still love you because your face is disfigured? How little you understand the heart of a woman —a real woman! Mr. Bridger, go into the next room. Margaret is waiting for you. She loves you— she has always loved you, and there has never been anyone else. You and she have things to speak of together.

"Afterwards, we shall discuss this matter on which you came to seek my advice. I think before we have finished we shall discover the truth about Mike Harrison. But that can wait; Margaret can't. Now go!"

And in obedience to Yvonne's command. Jim Bridger rose to his feet, looked at her wonderingly for a moment, brushed his hand across his tattooed forehead, then went stumbling across to the door which led to Yvonne's private room.

When it had closed after him, Yvonne laughed oddly, then she lit a fresh cigarette and dropped into Margaret Bryan's chair. For a long time she was silent, then her lips parted, and had one been close one might have heard her murmur:

"Fools and babies! As if outward disfigurement matters to a woman if she loves!"

Then she rested her head on her hand and sat waiting, while those two in the next room found their way through the jungle of suffering which they had entered through cruel misunderstanding.

End of Prologue.

THE STORY

MR. SEXTON BLAKE and his assistant Tinker had been in camp close to the Portuguese East African line —but on the British side — for just under a week.

And, although they had ostensibly arrived in the wild country for the purpose of shooting lion and smaller game, such as duiker and impala, not to mention the lordly kudu if they could dig up some sort of legitimate reason to defy the government ban on the "royal game," their bag was by no means heavy, so far. Several duikers and impala, one rather mangy-looking old lion, a couple of zebras, and innumerable wild dogs, which had been shot to clear them away from the camp rather than for sport, was about all they had to show for their efforts.

It was not because it was not good game country. On the contrary, the place was excellent for sport, and as their camp had been pitched a bare half-mile from Umbala's kraal, a fierce old Zulu with whom they were on the best of terms, there had been no scarcity of beaters.

But, curiously enough, and indeed, somewhat to the puzzlement of the men of Umbala's kraal, the white men made no effort to push matters. They did not even attempt to hunt every day, although Umbala's hunters appeared regularly with vivid tales of what they could show the "baas" if he would but accompany them. Sometimes the big baas and the young baas did so, but as often as not they declined, and simply spent their time about the camp.

The truth of the matter was that Sexton Blake did not want to pile up too big a bag, for, if he did so before he was ready to break camp and return south, the real business which had brought him there would not have been carried out.

He was playing a patiently waiting game; and none knew better than Blake that in this lay his only hope of success.

While neither Umbala nor any of his men suspected the true reason for the white man going into camp close to the Portuguese border, Blake's Hottentot "boy," Toby, knew a little of the truth, and, as his baas had treated him far better than many former masters, it was Toby's proud duty to render, as he thought, mighty assistance to his baas.

Why Blake and Tinker were there is briefly told.

16

Some two months before, Sexton Blake had been visited at his consulting-room in Baker Street by an elderly lady who had exhibited signs of great distress. The cause had been serious trouble which her son, who was in South Africa, had got himself into.

From what she told Blake, it appeared that the young fellow had gone out to South Africa about a year before and had taken up a small farming property in Southern Rhodesia, not far from Salisbury. He had apparently been doing as well as could be expected when, like a thunderbolt, came the news of his trouble.

He had been arrested on two counts —one for selling liquor to the natives, and the other for illicit diamond buying. After his arrest he had written one letter to his mother, in which he had stoutly affirmed his entire innocence, and had maintained that he had been the victim of a trap by which others, who were really guilty, had escaped.

Whether this was so or not, of course Sexton Blake did not know, but, at the earnest behest of the young fellow's mother, he had agreed to go out to South Africa as soon as his affairs would permit, and see what he could do.

As soon as he had got things straightened out in London, he and Tinker had sailed for Cape Town; and on his arrival there Blake had discovered that Tom Seagrave, the young man in question, had been sentenced to ten years on the Breakwater at Cape Town.

Through the influence he possessed, Blake had managed to secure an interview with Seagrave, during which Seagrave had told him what he knew of the affair, and also whom he suspected of having laid the trap for him. He had been guilty of mixing up with certain not very desirable characters in Salisbury, but that had apparently been the worst he had done.

And at the end of the interview Blake had believed him. Blake was convinced that there had been an unfortunate miscarriage of justice.

Unfortunately, the laws of South Africa relating to the traffic in diamonds is of such a nature that it is possible for innocent persons to be charged under it. Its purpose is good, and it has been designed to protect what is one of the most valuable industries of the country. At the same time; the very possession of diamonds which cannot be accounted for under the law is liable to lead to arrest and conviction, and this is just what had happened to Tom Seagrave.

Unquestionably the stones which had been found on him when he had been searched had been planted in his pocket by the man who had laid the trap; but the fact that they were found, and that he could give no satisfactory account for having in his possession four stones which were known to be illicit, had sealed his fate.

But he had given Sexton Blake the name of the man he suspected, and Blake had gone north determined to track the man down if possible, and when he had found him, to entrap him in some way into making a confession.

That was not going to be an easy matter by any means, and Blake knew it. Nor, when he got traces of the man at the small mining town of Speyfontein, did the problem look any easier.

It didn't take him very long by the methods he employed to ascertain that Thad Harker, the man in question, was quite capable of doing what Tom Seagrave had censed him of doing. Blake dug up several things which revealed a shady past, but, from what he could gather, Harker was the creature, and under the protection of certain powerful mining interests, for whom, it was said, he had carried out many questionable deeds.

But for some time Harker had been missing from his old haunts, and it took a great deal of patient probing on the part of Blake and Tinker to discover that he was then in Portuguese East Africa. They heard of him at Laurenco Marques, and then later news advised Blake that he had departed for the interior of the country.

That didn't look very promising.

While he remained in Portuguese territory he was perfectly safe. Blake hadn't anything sufficiently definite to justify him in swearing out a warrant and applying for the man's extradition to British territory. But through the assistance of the outposts of the Mounted Police he finally heard that Harker seemed to be making towards the border of Portuguese East.

It was just about then that he had taken the Hottentot boy Toby into his service, and he soon discovered that Toby could find out an astonishing number of things from the other boys in Speyfontein.

And it was through Toby that he learned of something that caused him to make sudden arrangements for a shooting trip into the Zululand country, from which he proposed making his way to the Portuguese East border.

This information was to the effect that one Gilbert Harrison, son of the well-known gold and diamond mining magnate, Sir Michael Harrison, was about to leave on a long trek north. Blake had known for some time that it was the Harrison protection which sheltered Harker, and, from one or two things which Toby also told him, he suspected that Gilbert Harrison might be going north to keep a secret rendezvous with Harker.

Men made no bones about discussing the Harrisons and the questionable means they had employed to get control of the great mining properties which had made them wealthy, but there was none brave enough to make his statements openly, and, whether they were true or not, the Harrisons were a power in the land, and Sir Michael one of the greatest political forces in South Africa. If there was any truth in the rumours, the magnate had taken good care to cover up all traces of his doings, and in his son Gilbert he had one who was as cunning and as ruthless as himself —or, rather, as ruthless, but not quite so cunning, as future events were to prove.

Blake did not wait for Gilbert Harrison to start north. He knew that, did he allow the other to start and then follow him, it might easily rouse the other's suspicions. Therefore, he and Tinker started first, and made no attempt to follow Harrison's movements until they were approaching the border of Portuguese East Africa.

Then, however, Toby had been sent back to follow the movements of the other party, and as he had once been in the service of Gilbert Harrison, as his back still showed the marks of a terrific sjamboking which Harrison had given him, it is easy to imagine that the Hottentot boy was only too eager to do what he could for the stern but kindly baas he now served.

Blake found him a perfect genius in tracking. Day after day he must have covered more than a score of miles, but each night he never failed to turn up at the camp before Blake turned in to report the exact whereabouts of Gilbert Harrison.

Then one night he had informed Blake that a boy had left the Harrison camp and was heading towards Portuguese East Africa. Blake had dispatched Toby after the other boy, while he himself opened up negotiations with Umbala, whose kraal they were then approaching. Umbala had supplied him with men, and eventually Blake had pitched his camp on a high spot half a mile from the kraal, and less than a hundred yards from the border of Portuguese East.

Two days later Toby had returned to deliver a very interesting report. A white man whom he had seen at Speyfontein, and whom he knew had had many dealings with Gilbert Harrison, had set up his tent on the other side of the border, not a quarter of a mile from Blake's camp. Harrison had apparently been delayed, and was still about two days' distant, but still clearly making towards the border.

Blake was now convinced that he was coming to meet Harker, and he was determined that if Harker should cross the border he would get his hands on him before he could get back. But Blake thought it unlikely that Harker would risk crossing. Something serious must have caused him to flee to Portuguese East, and the fact that he had pitched his camp on that side of the border showed that he was afraid to trust himself on the British side of the line.

The only solution seemed to be to try to lure him over the line in some way, and that was the problem over which both Blake and Tinker had been puzzling for several days while they hunted in a desultory fashion.

They had had one glimpse of Harker, and from the description he had received from Seagrave, and also in Speyfontein, Blake knew there was no doubt that he was the man he sought. That glimpse had been one evening when, guided by Toby, he and Tinker had crept across the veldt and had lain in the shadows outside Barker's tent watching him as he sat before the fire.

Of Harrison they had seen nothing, but on a certain night, after they had been in camp nearly a week, Toby had reported that Harrison had arrived and had pitched camp close to the border, but almost a mile away from where Blake and Tinker were encamped. That evening they had had a long discussion of ways and means.

For various reasons, Blake could not cross the border and kidnap his man. Such a move would only lead to complications, and, until he had something more definite to work on, Blake knew the folly of flouting the laws governing an international border line.

On the other hand, if it should take only a day or so for Harrison and Harker to complete their business, then Harker might slip though their fingers and make his way back in complete safety to Laurenco Marques.

The question was how to prevent that? They had thrashed out the problem for hours when Tinker had suggested putting the thing to Toby. Blake had consented, and the Hottentot boy had been called into the tent. Gravely Blake had explained their difficulty, and, to their surprise, Toby had put forward a solution without the slightest hesitation,

"By golly, baas, you want other baas come over line. Sure, very good, by golly, baas. Other baas shoot plenty all time. Every baas want more than anything shoot kudu, which king say not shoot.

"Umbala mighty induna, baas. Umbala know my baas a great baas. Umbala think plenty of my baas, by golly, yes. Umbala say kudu eat his crops. All white baas hear this. Umbala start many men out drive kudu along. All white baas want shoot kudu buck. By golly, that bring other baas over line. I think yes, by golly!"

Blake slapped his knee.

"I believe he has hit it, Tinker." he said with a laugh.

"Just what does he mean, guv'nor?" asked Tinker, who had not quite followed what Toby meant.

"Why, it is very simple. As you know, there is a perpetual ban on shooting the kudu because the animal is in danger of becoming extinct. The only exception made is when a headman can show that the kudus have been raiding his crops. Then it is allowed to shoot the buck leader, but no others. As soon as the leader is shot the herd makes off and doesn't return.

"That is what Toby says. It appears from what he knows, that our man is a keen hunter. Toby doesn't think he would be able to resist the chance to bring down a kudu buck.

"Therefore, he says, because Umbala is friendly to us that we can get him to proclaim that the kudus have been raiding his crops, and that means the buck may be shot. Then Toby says we should get Umbala to send out a large number of his men to drive up the herd, and by strategy have it guided along close to the border. In the meantime, word will be sent to any white men near at hand that a kudu drive is on, and, of course, Harker will hear of it.

"If he is as keen a shikari as the Hottentot says, then it is quite possible that, in the excitement of the moment, he might come across the border without knowing it, and then would be our chance if we were on hand. We would have to sacrifice our chance of bringing down the kudu buck, but Harker is bigger game for us.

"I believe this kinky-headed savage has thought of a plan worth trying. At any rate, I shall ride over to Umbala's kraal in the morning and see what the old man thinks of it. I believe I can trust him, and I shall take him into my confidence."

"It sounds all right, guv'nor," said Tinker, with a grin. "Toby's plan ought to work in his own country. But it all depends on just how keen a hunter Harker is."

"Quite right. The whole thing hinges on that, but in the absence of any other plan I think it is worth trying. We must make some move before Harker finishes his business with Harrison and gets away. Incidentally, I would give something to know why Gilbert Harrison has travelled all this distance to have a secret interview with such a shady character as Harker? I fancy it would be interesting."

Blake dismissed Toby, then, after some further discussion, Tinker turned in while Blake settled back on his cot to read for a little before snuffing out the candle. The tent was not a very large one —of oblong shape, some eight feet by five feet.

On one side was Tinker's cot, on the other was Blake's, and between them, at the head, was an empty packing-case which did duty as a table. It was on this that the candle stood by which Blake was reading, and from the outside his silhouette was plainly visible against the canvas; likewise Tinker's on the other side of the tent.

Tinker was already asleep, and Blake was just thinking about tossing the book aside when suddenly, without the slightest warning, it was jerked violently from his hand, and on the same instant came the sharp crack of a firearm outside.

Blake acted on instinct. Like a flash he realised that the book had been knocked from his hand by a bullet, and in that same flash he knew that the silhouette of his head had been the mark.

Scarcely had the book struck the ground when Blake hurled himself on the cot sweeping the candle from the top of the packing-case as he did so, and in the next action dragging Tinker to the ground beside him.

Tinker, who could not understand what it was all about, started to struggle, but Blake pushed him back.

"Keep still!" he ordered. "Someone took a snap-shot through the tent, and the bullet struck the book I was reading. We will go after him in a few moments, but wait until we see if there is a second shot."

They lay quiet, listening, but as Toby's voice came from outside the flap they struggled to their feet, felt in the darkness for their revolvers, then, throwing the flap aside, questioned Toby. All the Hottentot boy could tell them was that the sound of a shot had woke him up, and he had come to the tent to see what was the matter.

As he ran along he had seen the light extinguished, and he had feared one of them had been accidentally shot. Rapidly Blake explained what had occurred, pointing towards the spot from which the bullet must have come.

"By golly, we go quick, baas, we catch him!"

Blake agreed, and the next moment all three were racing towards the low belt of scrub where the marksman must have been concealed.

Twisting their prisoner's arms behind his back, Sexton Blake dragged him up. "Who are you?" asked the detective. "Light a match, Tinker, so that we can see." (*Chapter 2.*)

IT was well for Blake and Tinker that they had Toby to guide them through that dense belt of scrub, for without him it would have been impossible for them to penetrate more than a dozen feet, experienced shikaris though they were, without finding their passage barred by the prickly bushes and short, sword-like grass which formed the undergrowth.

Even in the open veldt it was none too easy finding one's way, even with the star-studded African night sky above, for, owing to the almost imperceptible miasma which rose from the tsetse level below the camp, things took on a blurred shape which was confusing.

But the Hottentot boy was worried not at all by the density of the bush. It might have been high noon, with the sun at its zenith, for all the trouble it gave him.

With the uncanny tracking sense of the bush Hottentot, he dodged about this way and that, choosing, apparently by instinct, the invisible openings among the bushes. Blake and Tinker kept close at his heels, for they knew by so doing was their only chance of making any progress. Besides, it was lion country there, and it is not wise to wander about alone too far away from the camp fire.

Off in the distance the wild dogs were making an infernal racket over some kill, and that was enough to bring the king of beasts loping across the veldt from miles away once he knew what was afoot. Not until a harsh menacing cough interrupted the feast would the wild dogs know of his presence, and then chaos would break loose.

It wasn't exactly the sort of party a man cares to invite himself to at midnight on the African veldt.

They had penetrated into the scrub for perhaps forty or fifty yards when suddenly Toby drew up abruptly, bringing Blake and Tinker on top of him in collision, for they had been unable to see his uplifted hand. When they had recovered they stood in silence, listening, and then they discovered what the Hottentot's sharp ears had distinguished. Ahead of them, somewhere, was the sound of crashing, as if some animal was dashing recklessly through the bushes. But Toby said:

"Him no animal, baas. By golly, we catch him man. We find now who shoot at the baas."

With that he started on again, and, as they progressed farther, even Tinker and Blake could hear the noise of the person ahead, who was floundering through the scrub like the veriest novice.

It seemed inconceivable that it could be a white man, and yet it was equally unthinkable that a native would dare to take such a pot-shot at a white man as had been taken at Blake.

On the other hand, no black would make such a racket as was being made by the man ahead. Had he done so, he would have been killed out of hand by his tribe to hide the shame. And not many white men who knew the veldt would be guilty of such tenderfoot folly. Nevertheless, Toby maintained that it was a man and not a beast, and knowing the Hottentot as he did, Blake accepted the statement without question.

But who could it be? he kept asking himself. Besides himself and Tinker, he only knew of two other white men who were camped anywhere near Umbala's kraal.

One was Barker, on the Portuguese side of the line, and the other was Harmon, whose camp Toby had reported as being about a mile from their own. It was conceivable that Harker, if he had got wind of why Sexton Blake was in that part of the country, might take a snapshot at him under cover of darkness.

But it was not easy to believe that one of his experience of the veldt would make such an awful hash of getting through the scrub at that hour of the night with all the beasts of the veldt out on the prowl. Nor could Blake suspect Harrison of the deed. What possible motive could he have for doing such a thing?

It was extremely puzzling, but, because Blake felt dead certain the bullet which had whipped the book out of his hand had been no haphazard shot, he was determined to run the marksman to earth if possible.

Then all of a sudden the noises stopped; but a few moments later they broke out with renewed vigour, seemingly close at hand.

"Him fall down," announced Toby. "We run now, baas."

He started to trot, and Blake and Tinker kept as close as they could. Then Toby gave a shout, and broke suddenly to the right. Tinker heard a violent thrashing about almost at his feet.

Risking the thorny branches, he made a low tackle, and found himself gripping a pair of leather-encased legs which were doing their best to brain him. The next moment Blake came crashing down upon the tangle, and, with his added weight, the man underneath lay quiescent. Toby, who had landed astride his head, now got to his feet, and, twisting their prisoner's arm behind his back, Blake dragged him up.

"Now, then, come along!" snapped Blake. "We want to have a look at you, my friend."

"I —I say, who are you?" came the voice of the man through the darkness. "I can't see an infernal thing. I lost my torch, and have been floundering about in this beastly scrub for an hour."

"Who are you?" asked Blake. "Light a match, Tinker, so we can see."

"I am Gilbert Harrison," answered the other. And the next moment, as Tinker struck a match, they saw by the flame that it was indeed the son of the mining magnate. Still, Blake did not release his hold.

"I am quite prepared to believe what you say, and to show you your way back to camp after you give me an explanation of a certain incident, Mr. Harrison," he said coldly. "You may have lost your way, but I see that you still retain your rifle. Well, a few minutes ago, while I was lying on my camp bed, reading, someone fired a shot which missed me only by inches. Our investigations so far seem to point to you as being the author of that attack. Why?"

"That is quite correct," answered Harrison readily enough. "I was trying to locate myself when I stumbled, and my rifle went off accidentally. I had no idea it had gone in the direction of anyone. I did not even see your camp. I swear that is the truth.

"Believe me, I am very sorry indeed that my carelessness should have put your life in danger, I am sure you will accept my regrets. If you will tell me your name, I shall make it a point to come across to your camp in the morning and explain more fully."

Blake released his arm. He was puzzled just what to say in reply.

The man's explanation had sounded straight enough, and, besides, what conceivable motive could he have for wishing to kill Blake? It was certainly a puzzler, and yet Blake would have wagered a fairly substantial sum that the bullet that had clipped past him so closely had been fired from a weapon deliberately aimed at his silhouette on the tent canvas. Still, what else could he say or do but make a show of accepting the apology?

"I accept what you say, Mr. Harrison," he said slowly. "It was a pretty close thing for an accidental shot. However, it did no harm, so no more need be said. My name is Blake, and I am in camp a short distance away. If you are lost, my boy will guide you back to your camp. It is, I understand, nearly a mile away, so you must have wandered considerably."

"I did," rejoined Harrison. "I started out just before dusk for a walk, and then got lost. I shouted to try to make my boys hear, but couldn't do so. I am not much of a bushman, but I thought I could find my way back all right. I couldn't, and I have been lost for some hours.

"I have been fighting through this scrub for an hour or more, I shall be very grateful to you if you will permit your boy to guide me back. And to-morrow I shall ride over and make a more suitable apology."

"I am riding to the kraal early in the morning," said Blake. "But if you care to, we should be pleased to have you ride over about midday and stay to lunch with us. I think Umbala is going to arrange a kudu drive, and, if he does, I presume you will want to take part."

"Oh, rather! I have never had a chance at a kudu. I shall certainly avail myself of your invitation, Mr. Blake. Can you manage to find your way back without your boy?"

"I think so. If we lose ourselves he will soon find us." Then Blake turned to Toby. "Take the baas back to his camp, Toby, and return as soon as possible. The young baas and I will find our way back alone."

Toby would have protested against his two masters going back alone, but in the darkness Blake gave his arm a sharp press, and the Hottentot remained silent. After a few more words, Toby started off, with Harrison at his heels, while Blake and Tinker began feeling a cautious way back to their own camp. They made no reference to the incidents until they broke through the edge of the scrub and saw the light of their campfire.

"Harrison confesses that he fired the shot, Tinker," said Blake, as they walked across the open ground. "We know that it must have been fired from very close to the edge of the bushes. And yet he said he didn't see anything of our camp. Now, what do you think of that, my lad?"

"I'll say that he is an active member of the Ananias Society," replied Tinker. "He couldn't have missed seeing our fire, guv'nor."

"That is exactly what I think, my lad. He also says he was lost.

Now, if we agree that he lied in his first statement —that is, if we take it that he did see our camp-fire— then, if he was lost, why didn't he come to our camp and ask us to put him right?"

"You've got me guessing, guv'nor. I can't figure him out."

"Nor can I —yet! That is why I invited him to come over for lunch to-morrow. I want to study the gentleman by daylight. And yet, if ever I heard sincerity in a man's apology, I heard it in his voice to-night, Tinker. I do not believe that he was trying to kill me, and yet — and yet —

"For a man that wasn't trying he made a pretty good job of it," grunted Tinker. "If he wasn't trying to kill you, guv'nor, then what was he trying to do? Answer me that."

"Um! rather a poser, my lad. But wait until Toby returns. We shall sit here by the fire and see what he has to say when he comes back. Things seem to be getting a little complicated around this part of the country; and, from all the signs, it looks as if we might get mixed up in them. I am very anxious indeed to know what business Harrison has with Harker."

Blake filled his pipe and sat smoking by the fire until there was a soft hail behind them. A few seconds later Toby came inside the circle of light.

"Everything all right, Toby?" asked Blake, glancing up at the black, who was showing his white teeth in a wide grin.

"All right, baas. I find him camp all right, by golly! That very funny, baas, him not see our camp-fire. What you think, baas?"

"Perhaps the bushes were too thick, Toby," answered Blake, who did not intend to commit himself to a criticism of the veracity of another white man, no matter how faithful the Hottentot might be.

"To-morrow morning I show you where him stand when him shoot, baas. I find that place easy, by golly!"

"All right. How many boys at the other baas' camp, Toby?"

"One —two —three boys, baas. One black feller I know, by golly, in Speyfontein. I talk with him before I come back, baas."

"Yes?" said Blake in an indifferent tone.

"Yes, baas. Him say that his baas send him across to camp of other baas this afternoon with message. Other baas bad man, baas. I know him, by golly! I work for Harrison baas one time, I tell you. This other baas he work for Harrison baas, too. Bad man, by golly! He sells bad whisky to kafir boy, baas."

"H'm! Harker seems to be a thoroughly bad case, Tinker," commented Blake in an aside. "It takes a pretty poor sort of a dog to sell liquor to the blacks. That may be why he is hanging out on the Portuguese side of the line,

"But I hardly understand his caution. I haven't heard of any of the Mounted being about this part of the country. But I suppose he is taking no chances. At any rate, it is interesting to know that Harrison sent him a letter to-day. I'd give something to know the contents. However, our main purpose isn't to discover what business there is between Harrison and Harker, but to lure that crook across to this side of the line if we can.

"And as old Umbala seems about the best bet in that direction, I shall ride to the kraal early. So let us turn in, my lad. I hope no one else will start taking pot shots at us during the night."

They rose, and said good-night to Toby, who promptly dropped down beside the fire. Blake led the way into the tent and lighted the candle. Tinker picked up the volume which Blake had been reading when the bullet tore it out of his hand.

They found that the lead slug had struck it fair in the back, and, after tearing a way through several pages, had glanced off. They searched about the ground for some time, trying to find it, and at last Tinker came upon it, lying on one corner half buried in the earth.

They found, on examining it, that it was undoubtedly of .401 calibre, but as Harrison had already confessed that he had fired it, there wasn't much to be gained by that discovery.

So they prepared to turn in.

But if Blake and Tinker could have been watching Gilbert Harrison at that same moment they would have been considerably enlightened on the mystery of the shot which had come so close to killing Blake.

IT is little wonder that Sexton Blake was puzzled over the mysterious secret rendezvous which Gilbert Harrison had undoubtedly made with Thad Harker.

It was unusual, to say the least, for a man of Harrison's position —for he was a figure of considerable importance in the financial life of South Africa, despite the insinuations cast against his father and himself as to how they had acquired some of their properties in the early days— to trek all the way from Speyfontein to the Portuguese border to hold a meeting with a known crook like Harker.

Only some very powerful incentive could have induced him to do so, and, if it proved nothing else, it did reveal that, in some way, Thad Harker must have been able to insist that Harrison come to him. That in itself was a tremendous confession of weakness on the part of Harrison, but only Gilbert Harrison himself knew the nature of the whip held by the man who had been a crooked tool for his father and himself for twenty years.

Gilbert Harrison had Boer blood in big veins from his paternal grandmother, and in him the full characteristics of the race had been stamped. He was a big man, very fat, with flat, round, placid-looking features which gave strangers the mistaken impression that he was not over-intelligent.

As a matter of fact, he was more cunning than shrewd, and while in his father's absence in England, he assumed full control of their interests in South Africa, he had displayed very little of the native sharpness which had enabled the older man to build up his large fortune and secure control of some of the richest gold and diamond mines in the country.

The elder Harrison had certainly used dubious methods at times, but he had taken very good care that no loose ends had been left sticking out. Therefore, the innuendoes cast by others left him cold. He was secure in the knowledge that, while they might talk, they couldn't prove anything against him.

If Gilbert Harrison had been content to play second fiddle to his father all would have been well, and he wouldn't have found himself skulking about the Portuguese East African line at that time instead of being in Speyfontein, where he should have been.

For his father was already on his way out from England, and

there were several matters it behoved Gilbert Harrison to cover up before the probing questions of his parent should uncover them. Gilbert Harrison owed his present position to an insatiable greed for money.

It is true that Sir Michael kept a pretty tight hold of the purse-strings for one of his great wealth; and it is equally true that sons of fathers far less rich than Sir Michael had a lot more money to play round with than did Gilbert Harrison. Nevertheless, he was paid what the ordinary man would have been highly satisfied to receive, and eventually he must come into the bulk of his father's fortune, for he was an only son.

Therefore, it was folly for him to have embarked on the various schemes which had been the bane of his life for several years—schemes which had been evolved by the fertile brain of Thad Harker, who had soon found the weak spot in Gilbert Harrison's nature.

For years this sort of thing had been going on, but Harrison had been lucky enough to keep the truth hidden from his father. That had been made easier owing to the fact that of late years the elder man had spent a large proportion of his time in London, where he was no little figure among the magnates of the City.

But recently everything that Gilbert Harrison had touched had proved disastrous.

His stock gambling had eaten up a very large sum. Other ventures had proved equally fatal, and, aside from the fact that he had defrauded two men out of their diamond claims —one of whom was Jim Bridger, who had been "railroaded" to the Breakwater in Cape Town —he had not been clever enough to bring off the frauds without leaving a good deal of incriminating evidence lying about.

And, to make matters worse, that evidence was in the hands of Thad Harker, who on the strength of it, had been blackmailing him for months past for ever-increasing sums.

And, hot on the news that his father was coming out from England, Thad Harker had made another demand —a demand for such a large amount that it meant certain disaster to Gilbert Harrison to meet it.

Sir Michael would have forgiven him for securing further diamond claims by dubious methods; he would not forgive him for being so clumsy as to leave incriminating evidence about.

Sir Michael had assumed a very devout respectability with the title which he had managed to secure, and the son knew just how terrible his rage would be if anything should come up now to besmirch that title. The old man would have forgiven, too, any moderate losses which the son had incurred, or any necessary sums spent to secure the claims, but he would never forgive the son for allowing himself to be placed in a position where a man of the stamp of Thad Harker could blackmail him.

And, above all, he would never forgive the vast sums which the son had taken secretly from the funds of which he had been guardian; for over a period of ten years those sums had mounted and mounted, until now they had reached the staggering total of nearly fifty thousand pounds.

Gilbert Harrison knew that by luck and cunning he might have been able to keep things covered up until his father returned to England. That had been before the last demand made by Harker. This demand had been for the modest sum of five thousand pounds, and had been couched in terms which Gilbert Harrison could not ignore.

On the other hand, it was utterly impossible for him to meet the demand without precipitating disaster. To do so he would have to dispose of further securities, and there were none available that he could lay his hands on. Those now in his possession were of such a nature that they would come under the immediate inspection of his father on his arrival.

If he could weather that first inspection he knew he had a pretty good chance of still keeping things quiet, for if his father found the major securities all in order, it was unlikely that he would take the trouble to check up the minor holdings. But if he found anything suspicions, he would have a thorough house-cleaning, and no one knew that better than Gilbert Harrison,

He had borrowed to the limit of his credit. Indeed, those loans were an additional source of worry to him, for some of his creditors had hinted that they would like to be repaid. He had held them off with promises, and, as they felt secure enough in the fact that he was Sir Michael's son and heir, they were not inclined to be really troublesome.

But Harker he could not ignore.

The man held enough material not only to ruin him, and send him to prison for a long term, but he could also bring the old man into the dust. And he was the only man living who held that knowledge.

Would Sir Michael ever forgive his son for permitting those loose ends to lie about to be picked up by Thad Harker? Never!

Yet Harker was insistent. On the other hand, Gilbert Harrison simply dared not realise on any more securities. He had cast about in every direction for a way out, but had failed to find one.

He had pleaded with Harker to wait until his father should return to England, when he promised to find the five thousand pounds.

But Harker had only laughed.

If Gilbert did not hand over the money by a certain date, then Harker threatened to go to Sir Michael as soon as he reached Speyfontein, and expose everything. That was the position when Harker slipped off to Portuguese East Africa and sent his final ultimatum. There was nothing for Harrison to do but to meet him.

But he came to the border-line without the money. He had been unable to raise it, and, in a fury of helplessness at the corner into which Harker had driven him, he had determined to kill the other man and end the business once and for all.

Gilbert Harrison was not a physically brave or courageous man. But even a rat will fight desperately when it is cornered, and it was the fury of despair that was driving him on.

He would meet Harker; he would promise him anything; he would watch his chance, and then he would kill him. That was the decision which Gilbert Harrison had come to when he had pitched his camp near Umbala's kraal.

And no man had ever been more astounded than Gilbert Harrison when, as he was floundering panic-stricken through the scrub, he had been brought down by Sexton Blake, Tinker, and the Hottentot.

For Gilbert Harrison thought until that moment that the shot he had fired from the concealment of the bushes had killed Thad Harker, for whom it had been intended.

Not until then had he known that he had made a mistake in locating the camp. Owing to the nature of his errand, he had been unable to take one of his boys with him to show him where Harker's camp was situated. He had not heard of the other white man's camp, and, after wandering about for some hours trying to find Harker's camp from vague directions given him by the boy he had sent to Harker's that afternoon, he had stumbled on Blake's.

He had skulked about for some time at the edge of the bush trying to nerve himself to the deed.

In him was a shivering fear of the consequences if he should fail, and if Harker should discover the truth. But driving him on was the greater fear of what discovery would mean, and so when he had seen the silhouette of a man's head against the tent canvas he had taken it for Harker's.

He had aimed as carefully as he could, then as he pulled the trigger he had seen the silhouette suddenly disappear, and the light go out. He had concluded that the bullet had found its mark, and that, in falling, the body had struck the candle, knocking it to the ground and extinguishing it.

A natural conclusion, but wrong, as he discovered later.

Then he had turned; and, in a panic, had dashed back through the bush, making for any place, so long as it took him away from Harker's camp. And now Gilbert Harrison sat in his tent, re-reading the letter which Harker had sent him that afternoon and trying to think of some way by which he could still free himself of the incubus which was bearing him down to ruin.

But how to do it?

That was the question that was driving him to the verge of insanity.

For one moment it came to him that even now he might find his way to Harker's camp and shoot him down in his sleep. But he still retained sense enough to realise the folly of that after the way he had already muffed things.

If Harker were found shot the man Blake would be almost certain to think it odd after what had happened at his own camp, and while Harrison had no idea that the "Mr, Blake," whom he had almost killed in error was the famous criminologist, Sexton Blake, the fact that he was a white man made the thing too risky.

The manner in which he had received Harrison's explanation marked him as a man of considerable decision of character, and one who was not to be fooled by any such play as that. And yet, something had to be done. Harker's letter of the afternoon made that definite.

For the twentieth time, Harrison took it from his pocket and read it again: —

"Dear Mr. Harrison (it ran),

"I have received your letter and I am pleased that you have come to meet me as requested. I regret, however, that you seem disinclined to accommodate me in the matter of the loan. However, I am quite sure that you will change your mind on reflection.

"Therefore, I shall expect a visit from you to-morrow evening to complete matters. Of course I am quite sure that your father would be pleased to accommodate me if I should approach him in the matter, but as we have already had so many dealings together in the past, I prefer that the transaction should be with you.

"I am anxious to return to Laurenco Marques, as I intend sailing for England at an early date, so I am quite sure you will not disappoint me. I might mention that on the completion of the loan I shall be pleased to hand over to you certain papers which I possess, and which I believe will prove of some value to you. —Yours,

T. H."

There, it was —as rank a piece of blackmailing as one could imagine; so certain did Harker feel of his victim that he had not even taken the trouble to be cautious.

If Harrison had had the nerve to face things out he could have sent the man to the Breakwater for ten years just on the last sentence alone, but he did not have the nerve, for the simple reason that an exposure would send him to the Breakwater as well. And that he could not face.

"There must be some way," he said desperately; then checked himself as he found that he had voiced his thoughts aloud. "Some way —some way," he kept thinking. "It can't be so risky away up here in this wilderness as it would be nearer a settlement. If I could get this man Blake out of the way I could work it.

"No matter what Umbala might suspect, his story wouldn't have any weight. I could fix that all right. But I must do it and get back before the old man arrives. If I don't, I am finished. But how to do it? There must be some flaw in Harker's defences through which I can get him— some trap that I can lay for him."

He fell into a brooding silence then, and for a long hour he did not stir. From the tense expression of his countenance it was plain that his mind was feverishly probing every avenue of possibility, and at the end of an hour a new expression came into his eyes.

"It might work—it might work," he whispered. "I can try it at least. I shall know when this man Blake comes back from the kraal in the morning. Harker might fall for it —he is a keen enough shikari tp do so, if he doesn't suspect a trap.

"I'll send him a letter in the morning telling him that I will make him the loan and mention in it that there is going to be a kudu drive. If this fellow Blake doesn't fix it up with Umbala I will do so myself. Yes —it is the only way. I must kill him —I must!"

With that he cast himself down on his camp bed and fell into a troubled sleep. There were too many fantastic pictures hashing across the retina of his brain for him to dispense with the friendly light of the candle.

Gilbert Harrison was in a deep hole, and he was plunging to greater depths in the desperate decision he had made —for the morrow was to bring a startling denouement.

Kudo /drf

SEXTON BLAKE got away early the next morning on his way to Umbala's kraal, and, on his arrival, found the induna pleased to see him.

As a warrior Umbala had been one of the mightiest of the Zulus, and during the Zulu war no chief had fought more bravely than Umbala. He was a chief feared and respected among his people, nor had the weight of many years and much avoirdupois served to vitiate his authority in the slightest. He was a very shrewd savage, and a keen judge of men.

It had taken him a very short time to place Sexton Blake in his true category, and because the chief saw far too few men of Blake's stamp and far too many of an undesirable type who bedevilled his people and sold them bad whisky, he had extended a warm welcome to Blake.

Which made things very agreeable for Blake and Tinker in that country where the whole success of their mission rested on the friendship of the ruling chief.

But, while Blake received a gracious welcome, he found the chief to be a very harassed old gentleman.

But it was not until Blake had made his greeting that he discovered the real cause of Umbala's bad temper. Then it became all too evident, for from the big hut before which he sat there issued forth a babel of shrill voices which told Blake that Umbala's numerous wives were having domestic argument.

Now Blake did not know until afterwards that quite lately Umbala had very foolishly taken unto himself an additional wife —a comely young maiden whose complexion was of a most desirable shiny ebony, and whose kinky hair had fascinated the eye of the chief.

It was an unwise move on Umbala's part, but nevertheless revealed no little courage, for it was well known that although he was certainly mighty among men, he was as a leaf of the forest among the women of his household, who were continually bickering among themselves and making the old man's life a misery.

Some day they would go too far, and Umbala would devastate them, as could be done in the good old days. But until that time should come, he was having a rough passage of it, and his domestic barque had not found smoother water when he had presented his latest acquisition to an indignant circle of dusky ladies, who ranged in age all the way from sixty-five to seventeen.

And so, in order to try to get a few minutes' peace from the racket, he had betaken himself outside to make his own voice heard where it was listened to with proper respect.

As it happened, Blake could not have chosen a better moment to suggest a kudu drive, for excitement of some sort was just what the old gentleman was pining for, and in Blake's suggestion he found the solution.

After the preliminary greetings were over Blake produced a large tin of chocolates, which he had brought as a gift. Umbala did not smoke, nor did he drink, but he had a passion, for sweet things, and a tin of chocolates such as Blake produced was enough to send him into a senile ecstasy of delight.

Moreover, he could consume the whole lot while the white man visited with him, and thus none of his wives would be able to snatch a single one away from him.

Yes, after all, things might be worse. His wives were still quarrelling, it was true, but then the sun was shining hotly, the white man was an agreeable companion, and he could listen lazily while he consumed the chocolates. And he would put from his mind all thought of the reckoning which might come later —not only from his wives, but also from his stomach, which did not share his palate's fondness for large quantities of sweet things.

On second thoughts, he decided to be daring, and save two —just two of the chocolates for his newest and favourite wife. She was a dusky lady of determined character, and he fancied she would reciprocate by keeping off the pack.

So with this generous thought, the old gentleman gave ear to what his visitor was saying.

Strictly speaking, the crops of Umbala's people had not been molested by the kudu herd, although there was a large herd a short distance away, as Blake knew from the reports of the native scouts who came to the camp frequently.

But he knew the cunning old savage would find no serious obstacle in that, for it could be arranged with very little trouble that some of the crops should be found to have been eaten by stragglers from the herd.

To the usual visitor Umbala would have given a curt refusal, but he had found this particular white man more of the type he had known in the past than those he had met of recent years, and that meant a lot.

Therefore it did not take very much persuasion on Blake's part to get Umbala to agree, and as soon as that was done his son was summoned.

This young warrior, a stalwart such as Umbala must have been years before, received the news eagerly, and, squatting down, proceeded at once to form definite plans with Blake. They talked the matter over for a couple of hours or more, then, when Blake had partaken of a large gourd of milk, he took a ceremonious departure.

Umbala seemed loth to let him go, for the chocolates were about finished now, and there was an ominous silence in the hut of the chief. But Blake had no intention of being a witness to any domestic humiliation which might fall upon the aged warrior, so he managed to get away before the storm broke.

He rode back to camp in high spirits, and on his arrival, found Tinker and Toby busily engaged in cleaning weapons. Toby was not trusted with a firearm, but he was allowed to assist in the cleaning, for the very sight of a gun sent him into an ecstasy of delight.

Blake imparted his news to Tinker, and had just finished when half a dozen of Umbala's young men arrived to receive instructions. Among them was Umbala's chief hunter, and, in order that there might be no mistakes made, Blake went over every detail two and three times.

Now Blake's camp was situated on a level bit of ground well up above the tsetse and fever level. That was one reason why it had been selected, the other reason being because close at hand was an old stone kraal, small, but quite secure from lions, and therefore convenient for turning the horses into at night.

Off to the right, and barely a hundred yards away, was the nearest point of the Portuguese East African border line. To the north was the belt of scrub from which Gilbert Harrison had fired into Blake's tent. To the west, across undulating veldt, was the way to Umbala's kraal; and to the south more veldt, with a small kopje in the far distance.

It was to the north-west that the kudu herd had been reported— that is, in a direction midway between the trail leading to Umbala's kraal and the direct line through the belt of scrub. Beyond that scrub, about a mile distant, was Gilbert Harrison's camp, and to the east, not more than a quarter of a mile by crow flight, was Thad Harker's camp.

Close to the edge of the belt of scrub, on the eastward side and stretching across the border line, was a miniature coulee, or shallow gorge, about a hundred yards or so in width, and stretching north for a matter of a couple of miles.

It was that shallow depression which Blake had already fixed upon as most suitable for his purpose, and, when he had examined the spot, the chief hunter agreed with him.

This savage did not know just why Blake wanted the herd of kudu driven along this depression, but that condition did not make him curious, for it was a really excellent spot for the drive.

Next came the discussion of the time, and, on the recommendation of the chief hunter, an early hour for the following morning was set. Scouts had already been sent out to locate the kudu herd, and when their reports had been received, a large number of Umbala's men would start out during the night and quietly surround the herd. Then, just before daybreak, they would begin to close in, and by sunrise the herd would be started towards the upper end of the coulee. On the other side, more of Umbala's men would be posted, so that once the leader struck the depression, he could be sent south. Once he was started, the whole herd would follow him.

It was Blake's intention to suggest to Gilbert Harrison that he post himself on the west side of the depression about a hundred yards from their camp. Then he hoped that when news of the drive reached him, Thad Marker would take up a position on the east side.

The border line dipped right down into the coulee there, and, if he could only get Harker planted close to it, Blake thought that, with Tinker on the same side and himself just opposite, they might catch Barker napping.

As an added precaution Toby would be placed close to Tinker, and they would both be charged to act swiftly should Harker cross the line. There is a good deal of excitement in a kudu drive, and Blake was counting on this to cause Harker to forget for the moment that he was so close to the line.

Toby was charged to keep his own counsel and not to ask why he was being instructed to attack a white man, Blake promising him immunity from any punishment.

As the Hottentot boy had a very old grudge against Harker, he was only too delighted at getting a chance to attack him under the protection of his present powerful baas, and, from the gleam of his white teeth, Blake knew that if Harker crossed the line anywhere near where Toby was posted, he would have a slim chance of getting back again.

Then Gilbert Harrison turned up as promised, and from Blake's reception of him it was impossible to guess that his explanation of what had happened the previous night had not been accepted quite at its face value.

He looked a wreck in the strong light of middle day. His eyes were bloodshot and sunken, his face was flushed, and his mouth was slack.

As they shook hands, Blake detected the odour of whisky on his breath, and, from the general appearance of the man, he knew something very serious was on his mind. But neither he nor Tinker gave any sign as they sat in the shade and chatted, while Blake described the success of his visit to Umbala, and the detailed plans he had made for the drive early the following morning.

As he talked, Harrison seemed to brighten up considerably, and when Blake asked him if he would take up a post during the drive, he accepted with obvious eagerness. While Toby was cooking lunch, Blake, Tinker, and Harrison walked up the coulee until they were near the edge of the scrub. Then Blake came to a pause, and, pointing towards the north, said:

"I have arranged for the herd to be driven along this depression towards where we are standing. With the buck in the lead, that should make it possible for one of us to bring him down as he passes, and it will also allow the rest of the herd to continue on and scatter across the open veldt to the south.

"If all goes according to plan, they ought to pass fairly close to your camp, but I think it would be better if you took up a stand near here. Unfortunately we are a man short. To be posted as I should wish, we ought to have four guns instead of only three."

"Exactly what is your plan?" asked Harrison quickly.

"It is this, as I have explained, the herd will come along this coulee, and it is certain that they will come at a terrific pace. My idea is for you to take up a position about there" —and Blake indicated a spot about forty yards along.

"You can be in the concealment of the bushes there, and you will be favoured by getting first shot at the buck. I, myself, will take up a position just here where we are standing, while this young man will be directly opposite me on the other side of the coulee.

"To complete the arrangement, we ought to have one more gun to take up a post opposite you. In that way we would be disposed strategically, and it is by no means sure even then that we will bring down the buck, for he will be travelling like greased-lightning. What do you think of the plan?"

"I think it is good —very good indeed —but I agree with you that another gun is needed. And I think I know where I can get that."

"Oh! That would simplify matters. Exactly what do you mean?"

"There is another man camped just across the line. I have a slight acquaintance with him, and I know him to be a very keen shikari. It just happens that I am going across to his camp this evening, and I could ask him then to join in. I believe he would accept."

"That would he excellent. I haven't met this man, but I am keen to wind up our shooting trip by bagging a buck kudu, if possible. If he will join us, will you tell him that the drive will start very early tomorrow morning, and it will be necessary for him to take up position before dawn?"

"Yes. Er —I suspect he will not be keen on crossing the border line. It is just near here, isn't it?"

"It is some place on the other side of this depression," replied Blake carelessly. "If he doesn't want to cross the line then, that will not matter. If he takes up a position about opposite you he will still be on the Portuguese side of the line, and still an effective gun." Then Blake smiled.

"We don't care what his reasons may be for wishing to remain on the other side of the border," he said. "I understand there are plenty of persons who prefer the hospitality of the other side, but if he is one of them he need not be afraid that we shall be curious. We are here to shoot and to bring down the game we came after, and I hope that we shall succeed in doing so to-morrow morning."

A sentence which, to Tinker, had more than one meaning, but which to Harrison seemed to refer only to the buck kudu.

They strolled back to the camp then, and most of the conversation hinged on big game hunting.

Had he not been so engrossed in his own affairs, and had his mind not been struggling with the problem of how to persuade Harker to take a hand in the drive the following morning, Gilbert Harrison would probably have shown more curiosity about Blake and Tinker, for he stated that he recalled having seen them in Speyfontein.

However, he did not ask any embarrassing questions as to the business which had taken them there, and be sure Blake did not enlighten him. Moreover, Harrison was so relieved at discovering that Blake had arranged the very thing that he most wanted that he could think of nothing else.

Harrison took himself off early in the afternoon, and as he watched the fat man lumber off, Blake nodded his head with satisfaction.

"The trap is set, my lad," he said. "Tomorrow morning we will spring it and see what we catch."

"We'll get more than the buck kudu, or I miss my guess," rejoined Tinker, with a grin. His words were to prove strangely prophetic.

" What is it? What has happened, my lad? " rapped out Blake as he dropped
to his knees and took in at a single glance that Harker was dead. " I
didn't do it, guv'nor," replied Tinker. The Hottentot was looking scared.
" By golly, baas, I saw him go down under the young baas. I think him shot
by other baas over there." (Chapter 5.)

THE first grey streaks of dawn were just rimming the eastern sky when Blake's camp was greeted by the spectacle of a small cavalcade approaching.

As it drew near, Blake and Tinker were able to discern the figure of Umbala huddled upon the broad back of one of the royal riding bulls, and behind him, likewise mounted, were four of his younger warriors as a guard. Blake had not known that the old man intended favouring his camp with his presence, so, giving hasty directions to Tinker to have a seat placed by the fire, he hastened forward to do the honours.

He assisted Umbala to alight, and then conducted him to the canvas camp-chair which Tinker had placed ready. The four warriors took up their position on the ground behind the chief, and then Umbala announced that he had come in order to be present at the kudu drive.

Technically he was in attendance in order to see that only the buck was killed, but in reality he was hoping for half of the buck to be given him as a present. Blake made a shrewd guess at the truth, but he was not displeased at Umbala's coming.

On the contrary, it fitted in very well indeed with his plans, for it would be as well, he opined, to have an independent witness of what might take place later on. As a matter of fact, as things turned out he was extremely glad that Umbala was there.

The old gentleman looked a little grey about the gills, and complained of having had a wretched night after his chocolate orgy. Tinker produced another large tin of the succulent sweets, but although Umbala eyed it longingly, he shook his head sadly.

Nevertheless, he graciously condescended to accept it for consumption later on, confiding it to the care of one of his warriors.

Just after Umbala arrived, Gilbert Harrison put in an appearance, and, after being presented to the chief, informed Blake that he had visited the camp of the other white man the evening before, and that he had accepted the invitation to join in the drive.

He did not look so haggard as he had on the previous day, but there was a feverish nervousness about him that told its own tale.

He had told the truth when he stated that he had visited Harker's camp the previous evening, but he did not add that only his solemn promise that he was expecting the money to arrive by special messenger within twenty-four hours had made it possible for him to stall off Harker.

It had been a stormy interview between the two men, one running the whole gamut from threats and curses to whining pleas, the other cold and adamant, yielding not an inch.

And if Gilbert Harrison had been inclined to waver in his resolve, that interview was sufficient to steady him.

They were still talking by the camp when they saw a black boy coming towards them. He spoke to Toby, who then informed Blake that the other baas was waiting at the edge of the coulee a short distance away, and would the baas walk along and show him where he was to take up his position? With a word of excuse to Umbala, Blake asked Gilbert Harrison to accompany him.

They strode down into the shallow depression, and made their way along until they heard a hail from the bushes on the right. As they turned and went towards the spot, Blake noted with considerable satisfaction that the almost invisible post marking the boundary line ran almost to the top edge of the depression at that spot. If he could manage to post Harker about there, it would only need a few incautious steps on his part to bring him over the line.

Harker broke cover as they reached the top of the depression and stood gazing at them. Blake sized him up swiftly from the low, sullen brow and the close-set, cunning eyes, to the too-heavy jowl and heavy physique of the human brute.

In that brief analysis of the man he was quite ready to believe all that Tom Seagrave had told him about Harker, and he was more intrigued than ever to know what could be the reason for Harrison coming all that distance for a secret meeting.

He noted, too, that Harrison seemed nervously anxious, almost cringing in his manner to Harker, which puzzled Blake all the more, for, as value went, the attitude should have been reversed, considering the relative positions of the men.

He made no attempt then to lure his quarry over the line. He knew that Harker was still on guard, and if he got suspicious now the whole thing would fall through. If he was as keen a shikari as was said, then Blake counted on the excitement of the drive as the buck came along to make him forget for a moment to be cautious.

Blake contented himself with merely discussing the details of the drive, explaining what he had arranged, assuring Harker that he was most anxious to add a buck to their bag before breaking up their shooting camp, and winding up by thanking him for joining in.

He spoke so straight, and so obviously thinking of nothing else but the drive, that almost perceptibly Harker's attitude relaxed.

He held himself more at ease, and, when he had studied the lay of the land, readily agreed that the spot Blake had chosen for him to take up his post could not be better. He asked directly where the others would be posted, but declined Blake's invitation to come down to the camp and take coffee before each went to his place.

He did not show any suspicion at the invitation, however, for it was given courteously as host to guest, Blake was not supposed to know that he did not want to come across the line, and, of course, Harker did not guess that the "Mr. Blake" who was on a shooting trip was "Sexton Blake of London."

He said very little to Harrison, and when the latter and Blake turned to go back to the camp Harker dropped back under cover.

After coffee Blake suggested that Harrison and Tinker take up their respective posts. As originally arranged, Harrison was to be on the left side of the depression, along with Blake, but about forty yards higher up. Almost opposite him was Harker, and on the same side as Harker was Tinker, though much nearer to Harker than Blake was to Harrison.

Then Blake gave a sign to Toby, who crossed the depression at Tinker's heels and disappeared from view.

His particular job was to work his way round quietly behind Harker, and then get in as close to him as possible without being seen. With the stage all set, Blake talked a few minutes with Umbala, then moved along and took up his own position.

It was impossible to tell how long they would have to wait. That all depended on where Umbala's scouts had located the herd, and how successful the others were in starting them on the drive. It might be half an hour, or it might extend to three or four hours. There was a clear view up the coulee for a good five hundred yards, and even if the yells of the beaters failed to reach them, there was plenty of time to spot the herd before it could come abreast of the guns.

As it turned out there was no danger of them not hearing the racket being made by the beaters, for, while the herd must have been fully a mile away, the noise reached them. Umbala's men seemed to be using every known contrivance, as well as their voices, to raise the most infernal din one could imagine.

It is little wonder, therefore, that when the magnificent buck stampeded with the herd behind him, every animal was travelling as Blake had prophesied —at a terrific pace.

From where he stood, Blake saw the leader come into view, then the herd of sixty or more appear as a leaping sea of yellow and white, their graceful heads held high in a frenzy of fear. Out of the corner of his eye he noted that Tinker had broken cover, and was moving rapidly along towards where Harker was waiting.

Blake gave a yell, and saw Harker wave his hand; then things began to happen so rapidly that one pair of human eyes could not take it all in.

Blake himself stood ready, waiting until the buck kudu got closer. He wanted to bring down the magnificent animal as much as any sportsman could want anything, but he wanted more to bag the human quarry he was stalking, and his attention was concentrated more on the human than the buck.

Tinker had made rapid progress towards the spot where Harker stood, and, as the herd got closer, Blake saw Harker break cover and step out to take a bead on the buck.

He glanced towards Tinker, and Blake saw him wave the lad back, but as he turned his attention once more to his sights Tinker covered another ten feet, which brought him almost within jumping distance of the other.

Still Harker had not crossed the line, although a bare six feet would carry him over.

So far Blake had seen no sign of Harrison, but he thought nothing of that, for just where he had taken up his post, the bushes offered considerable cover. It was Harker who fired the first shot, but his aim must have been bad, for the buck still came on. Harker pumped a fresh cartridge into the breech, and then ran out a few paces more to take a second sight before it was too late.

After him went Tinker, for Harker had crossed the line at last, and the lad was determined to bag him while he could.

Right behind Tinker Toby suddenly appeared, and, feeling pretty certain that the pair of them would be able to hold Harker until he got there, Blake took a quick sight at the buck and fired.

As he did so he saw a small puff of smoke from the spot where

Harrison lay, and the next moment the big buck leapt high in the air, then came crashing to the ground.

One bullet at least had found its mark.

Blake had already started to run towards the spot where Harker had stood. He had been just in time to see Tinker make a low tackle for Barker's legs before he fired at the buck, but now, as he ran on, he drew up with an exclamation of anger at what he saw.

Harker was lying on the ground with Tinker clinging to his legs, while Toby was just on the point of grabbing his arms. But Harker had rolled free, and seemed to be clawing for the heavy Service revolver which Blake had noticed in his holster.

Blake thought, of course, that Harker was trying to drag the weapon out in order to shoot Tinker, and, as the gun came free, he raised his own rifle to get in first shot. But even before he could do so Harker had made a violent movement, had heaved himself up, and, lying on his right shoulder, pulled the trigger three times in rapid succession.

Then he fell back, and Blake saw Tinker roll clear.

Completely at a loss to know what had occurred, Blake raced along until he reached the spot where Tinker and Toby were standing looking down at Barker's motionless body.

"What is it? What has happened, my lad?" rapped Blake, as he dropped to his knees and took in at a single glance that Harker was as dead as the buck kudu. "Don't tell me that you shot him."

"I didn't do it, guv'nor," answered Tinker, who appeared almost as puzzled as Blake "I haven't fired a shot this morning. I didn't know he had been hit until after I tackled him. It seemed to happen just as I brought him down. But he lasted long enough to pull his revolver out and do some shooting on his own account."

"I saw that," said Blake. Then he turned to Toby. "What did you see, Toby?"

The Hottentot was looking scared, but at Blake's words he made an effort to control himself. "By golly, baas, I see him go down under the young baas. I think him shot by other baas over there."

Suddenly Blake remembered that Harrison had not appeared. He ran up the other side of the depression, and plunged into the bushes where Harrison had been posted.

Lying huddled up on the ground was Harrison, and a brief examination showed that one of the bullets fired by Harker had struck him full in the heart.

"What a rough house!" muttered Blake. "Harrison shot Harker just as the buck got close to him, thinking he could say it was an accident. But before Harker died he killed Harrison. Both of them are gone, and, even now I don't know what it all means. But this must be straightened up, and at once. Thank goodness old Umbala was a witness to the whole thing!"

And with that Blake turned and strode back to where Tinker stood.

"THE first thing to see done is to get the bodies back to the camp," announced Blake as he reached Tinker. "You go along and tell Umbala what has happened. The chief won't approach here in an affair of this sort without being asked to. Say there has been an accident, and ask him to send his young men along to carry the bodies back. In the meantime, I want to have a look at the buck."

While Tinker hurried away Blake dropped to his knees and drew his hunting-knife. With Toby's assistance, he managed to turn the buck over; then he began searching for the bullet. He found it in the soft flesh at the back of the neck, just where it had lodged after breaking the buck's spinal cord.

Blake dug it out with the point of his knife, and, after a brief examination, dropped it into his pocket. Then he proceeded to make a minute examination of the whole of the carcass to discover if any other bullet had struck the buck. But when he finally desisted he was certain that the one he had already abstracted was the only slug which had reached the animal.

And that slug told him one thing beyond doubt. It told him that it had been his own shot that had brought the kudu down, for it was the bullet from a 30.30 cartridge, and his own Savage was the only rifle of that calibre in the party. A brief scrutiny had shown him that Harker had been using an old Springfield. Tinker, he knew, had employed a Winchester .38; and, from what had happened two nights before, he knew that Gilbert Harrison had favoured a Winchester automatic .401.

The next thing to find out was what calibre of bullet had killed Thad Harker, and that would have to wait until the bodies had been carried back to the camp.

As he rose to his feet, he saw that two of Umbala's men were already bearing the form of Gilbert Harrison along, and just then the other two came up at Tinker's heels. They lifted the body, and, followed by Blake and Tinker, carried it to the sleeping-tent.

Ordinarily, Blake would have greatly preferred that a doctor should probe for the bullet that had caused Harker's death, but as he knew there was not one within two hundred miles, it would have to be carried out by himself. Nor dared he delay too long, for in that climate the burial must be carried out without delay.

He amplified the description which Tinker had given to Umbala by explaining just how the "accident" had happened; and, while Umbala must have seen a good deal and must have suspected the double murder, he did not give a sign of what his thoughts might be.

If this white man of, obviously, a position of authority, was willing to call it an accident, why, then, so was Umbala. He had no desire to stir up any tiresome investigation, which would mean more white strangers invading his kraal. As a matter of fact, he was far more concerned about the fate of the buck, and was distinctly pleased when Blake announced that he would be honoured if Umbala would accept the whole carcass.

There would be no need to make even a brief post-mortem on Gilbert Harrison. Both he and Tinker had been actual witnesses of that, and their joint evidence would be sufficient in case of need. But in regard to Harker it was different.

Blake entered the tent alone, and, bending over the cot on which Harker lay, he began a cursory examination. It did not take him long to discover that the bullet had entered just under the left shoulder-blade, must have gone clean through the heart, then traversed either between or along the ribs to the right side, where it probably still was lodged, for Blake could find no signs of it having emerged from the body.

Working on this theory, he began at the right side, and, to his satisfaction, found what he thought must be the bullet just beneath the lower rib. At least, there was a suspicious lump there, and he decided to probe for it, and find out just what it was.

It was barely an inch in from the side, and a single slit of the knife revealed it to be as Blake had suspected —the bullet which had caused Barker's death. As he brought it forth Blake held it up; then he nodded his head slowly.

"Just as I thought," he muttered. "The bullet from a .401-calibre rifle, and Gilbert Harrison was the only man in the party with a rifle of that calibre. But if it will ever be known whether it was an accident or coldblooded murder depends on several things. For the time being I shall keep this discovery a secret between myself and Tinker."

On emerging from the tent, a nod from Blake was enough to tell Tinker what he had found; then he had another conversation with Umbala, in which it was decided that the chief should return to his kraal forth-with, and that some of his scouts should come to the camp for the dead buck.

He also promised to send other men to dig graves for the two dead white men. Blake and Tinker saw him off in full ceremony, after which they went back to the tent.

"What now guv'nor?" asked the lad.

"Harrison's camp first," answered Blake. "Then we will go on to Harker's. I must make an examination of their belongings, and arrange to take them back to Speyfontein with us. We will leave Toby in charge here."

The Hottentot was by no means anxious to remain alone at the camp, for he had a superstitious fear of what lay in the sleeping-tent. But his fear of Blake's stern eye was even greater, and when they started off up the coulee on their way to Harrison's camp, they left Toby, a dejected figure, by the ashes of the dead fire.

From the black boy they had received a pretty good idea of where they would find Harrison's camp, and, by following the instructions he had given them, they came upon it without difficulty.

It was typical of the lack of respect Harrison must have been held in by his "boys," for on the arrival of Blake and Tinker there was not one to be seen, and the whole camp was littered with bits of packing-case and empty tins. It was very different from the neat surroundings of their own camp.

A loud shout from Blake brought a sulky-looking black shambling into view, but at the crisp command in Blake's tones his attitude changed like magic. He knew the tone of authority of the real "baas," and answered it instinctively.

Blake explained that an accident had happened to his master, and that he and the young baas had come to the camp to take charge. He then sent him off to find the second boy, while he and Tinker entered the tent and began a systematic examination of Harrison's belongings. If they had expected to find anything there to throw any light on the mystery they were doomed to disappointment, for, although they missed nothing, they found not a single clue to explain the secret of the relations which had existed between Harrison and Harker.

When they had finished they went outside, where the two boys stood waiting. Blake gave curt instructions for them to get everything ready for a trek back to Speyfontein, then he asked which was the boy who had taken a letter to the camp of the white man across the border.

The one they had first come upon acknowledged that he had

taken the message, so Blake instructed him to lead the way.

They found that Harker had evidently been a much keener disciplinarian than Harrison, for, although his two boys were sullen and cowed in manner, the camp was as clean as their own, and had been pitched in quite as good a position. Here, as at the other camp, Blake made brief explanations, immediately after which he and Tinker set to work to go through Harker's belongings.

If they had been disappointed at finding nothing among Harrison's possessions, that was more than made up for by the packet of papers they found at the bottom of a tin in Harker's tent. Even a cursory examination revealed that they were of prime importance, and at the end of a quarter of an hour the secret that had lain between Harrison and Harker was theirs.

But, more than that, they had found the explanation of several matters in which Harker and Harrison had been mixed up, not least of which was proof that Tom Seagrave had told the truth in maintaining that he had been the victim of a plot.

In their possession were documents which Blake stated emphatically would clear the young man, and, now that their real purpose had been accomplished, Blake was all anxiety to get back to Speyfontein without any further unnecessary delay.

They had already spent more time on the case than they could easily afford at that time.

Leaving instructions with Harker's boys to get things ready for an immediate trek, but taking the valuable documents with them, they hastened back to their own camp. There they found that Umbala's men had arrived, and, under Toby's direction, were already busy digging the two graves. Blake and Tinker set to work, and with their own hands fashioned two rough coffins, for this was work that one white man must do for another.

And that evening, just before sunset, the two dead men, so similar in character yet so different in methods—gaining so little after years of crooked and criminal effort —were laid to their final rest in the lonely veldt, while Blake read a brief service over the open grave, and Tinker stood with bowed head in reverence of the great mystery which obliterates all the blackness of a man's evil life.

The two lonely graves were marked with plain wooden boards, and then piled high with stones to keep the wild dogs at bay. It was very late that evening before the work was completed, and after that their own camp had to be broken and their gear packed for the return trek. All hands worked straight through the night, and at dawn they were joined by Harrison's and Harker's boys, who were accompanied by several of Umbala's men bearing the camp gear. These same men had been lent to Blake for the down trek, and, after a quick round of coffee, the little cavalcade started on its way back to Speyfontein.

How little did either Blake or Tinker dream of the surprise which was awaiting them there.

" You haven't got them, ex-sergeant !" said Blake. Walters looked puzzled, and for a full half-minute gazed into the detective's eyes. " I said you haven't got them—for they are here !" Sexton Blake held up two uncut diamonds between his finger and thumb. (*Chapter 7.*)

SPEYFONTEIN is typical of the smaller mining centres to be found in South Africa and Australia.

Like others, it first came into being as a scattered camp following the discovery of surface or alluvial gold. On the petering out of these it degenerated into a dreary stretch of waste ground dotted from end to end with miniature craters where the cradles had stood, and with only a few old-time fossickers and Chinese making up its population.

But later on, when the deep mining boom came on the Rand, it was discovered that Speyfontein —or what was left of it —lay astraddle a winding ridge, which showed outcroppings here and there of gold-bearing quartz.

Drilling soon disclosed the fact that the possibilities of deep mining appeared far more promising than made evident by the hasty and wasteful placer mining which had gone before, with the result that the place was favoured with a second "rush."

In this second lease of life, however, the single or two-claim man did not exist. Only companies well financed by shareholders who could afford to wait a considerable time for returns on their investment, could finance deep mines, so those adventurous spirits who came either stayed to labour in the rapidly deepening shafts or drifted on to other fields.

In its new dignity Speyfontein was not satisfied to remain a littered and scattered camp as in the past. Rickety, shacks gave place to substantial buildings of stone. A bank was started, churches were built, hotels arose, and shops, with real plate glass windows, lined the main thoroughfare.

It was an ugly duckling of a town, and no amount of care would ever make it anything else. Nevertheless, it grew rapidly in importance, and with the amassing of wealth by its pioneers, such as Sir Michael Harrison and his colleagues, it began to sift itself out into cliques and circles, which were spoken of as "society."

There were even those who boasted of belonging to the "old families" of the place, and when a town reaches that stage, it is definitely and finally doomed as a progressive factor.

Sir Michael Harrison and his like did not scorn to take all the wealth the mines of Speyfontein and the surrounding districts would give them, but, one by one, they were identifying themselves more and more with the larger towns and cities to the south, or, as in the case of Sir Michael, following an ambition to become known as a figure of importance in London itself.

At the time of Sexton Blake's visit to Speyfontein, on the occasion of his search for one Thad Harker, the town consisted of a single long main street, at each end of which was a hotel —that at the eastern end being generally looked upon as slightly more comfortable than the other, although, truth to tell, there wasn't much to choose between them.

Then there was a second sort of semi-main street that ran at right-angles to the wider thoroughfare, and off which were several other streets given up to residences. It wasn't a well-laid-out town, it wasn't a clean town, it wasn't a pretty town.

But it did clear a tremendous lot of gold and diamonds in the course of the year, and as those two commodities gave it its excuse of existing, no one thought very much about civic beauty.

It was just dusk one evening when Sexton Blake and Tinker rode into town from the western end. As they had stayed at the hotel at that end of the main street on their previous visit, they naturally decided to put up there again, so almost immediately after entering the confines of the town they turned their horses into the yard at the rear of the hotel.

As Toby was thoroughly at home in the place, and, moreover, knew every boy there, he was perfectly competent to look after their kit, so, after slipping out of the saddle, Blake and Tinker walked stiffly towards the side entrance to the bar to get something to wash the dust out of their throats.

They noticed that a man in uniform had walked up the steps just ahead of them, he opened the door, and, entering, slammed it in their faces. He may or may not have seen them directly behind them.

"That particular member of the police force wants jacking up," said Blake as he laid his fingers on the handle. "He needs to be taught the rudiments, at least, of common courtesy."

"He certainly does!" growled Tinker. "He seems to think he owns the show."

Blake opened the door, and stepped inside. Then suddenly he paused, and when Tinker had squeezed up beside him, Blake closed the door.

The place was full of miners just in off the second shift at the mines, and it was plain that until a moment ago they had been crowded about the bar drinking. But now they had drawn away from it, and stood against the opposite wall, leaving a clear space between the police-constable who had entered and another man who stood at the far end of the bar.

A swift glance showed Blake that the constable was in the uniform of a private of the "Mounted," while the other man was dressed in riding-breeches and loose khaki coat.

His hat was drawn well down over his eyes so that it was not easy to see his features, but it was plain that the constable had had no trouble in recognising him, for he stood facing the other, a heavy Service revolver aimed steadily at his heart. He must have gone into action the very moment he entered the bar.

Blake and Tinker stood listening while he spoke.

"It's been a long time, Bridger," he was saying, "but I knew you would drift back one day. And when you come back here you come on the old game. At least, it's a pretty good gamble that you do so, just to be on the safe side, I am going to search you here and now."

The man called Bridger shifted his attitude the veriest trifle, but did not change his lounging attitude.

"You're a good guesser, Walters, aren't you?" he sneered. "You aren't forgetting what a mistake in the past cost you, are you? Every time you clap eyes on me you go into hysterics and accuse me of having illicit stones in my possession. I was snaked on that once, Walters, and you can take it from me I won't be snaked again. It will take a cleverer man than you to pin anything on me. Don't forget your lost stripes, Walters, and don't forget that you can't touch me now."

As Blake heard the name "Walters" a second time, accompanied by mention of the fact that at some time in the past the constable had been reduced to the ranks, he glanced at him sharply; then, with a touch on Tinker's arm, he moved leisurely to the bar, where he and the lad took up a position directly between the constable and Bridger

The constable had started to curse at Bridger, but as the two strangers cut off his view he jumped to one side, then he addressed himself to Blake.

"What do you think you are doing?" he snarled.

Blake turned and regarded him briefly; then he shrugged.

"I remarked just before I entered that you needed to be taught the rudiments of good manners," he said coldly, "I am doubly certain of that now. Nevertheless, I will answer your question as to what I am doing. I am standing at this bar here with the intention of getting a drink, if you will call off your melodrama for the time being and permit me and my companion to take one in peace."

There was a snicker as Blake turned back to the bar, and in an unruffled tone gave the order. The girl hesitated as she caught sight of Walters' lowering countenance, but Blake's cold gaze impelled her to do his bidding without delay.

The solitary man at the other end of the bar laughed outright, then he moved towards Blake and Tinker. But he had covered less than a yard when the constable had jumped towards him, and by the expression on his face it was plain that he meant business.

"None of that!" he snarled. "No handing over the stones to your confederate here, I told you, Bridger, that I was going to search you here and now, and I am going to! Miss," he said, turning to the barmaid, "in the name of the law, I ask you to leave the bar until I call you in again."

He waited until she was gone, then he said:

"I call everyone here to witness that this is a legal search I am making, and I warn you that any man who interferes will do so at his peril. Now then, Bridger, stand away from that bar and begin to strip."

Blake turned round and looked at the man called Bridger. As the other removed his hat and dropped it on the floor, Blake and Tinker could both see that his forehead was disfigured by heavy tattoo-marks, the object of which was not plain in that light. But Walters enlightened the general crowd.

"Look at him!" he crowed. "Look at his forehead! He didn't have all that tattooing done to make him beautiful. Not he! If you look underneath it you will see the I.D.B. brand! We got him once, and we'll get him again! Now, off with that coat, Bridger!"

"Hold!"

All eyes went towards Blake as he held up his hand and stepped forward.

"While I take it you have the authority to conduct this search in this way, constable, you are forgetting, one or two rights belonging to the man you accuse.

"You insinuated a few moments ago that I might be a confederate of his. I may state to these other gentlemen that I have never seen him before in my life. But I am quite conversant with the rights of a citizen, and in this instance I propose to see them enforced!"

Walters glared at Blake truculently, but growled:

"Well, what about it?"

"Just this, if this gentleman whom you accuse of being in possession of diamonds which have been illegally bought, then the question must first be put to him. If he denies it, but submits to a search, then you are at liberty to go ahead. But, at the same time, I do not think it would be out of place for him to make a very simple request of the person who does the searching."

"What request? What are you getting at?"

"Wait!" Blake turned to Bridger. "Are you willing to undergo a search?"

"If it's on the level —yes."

"In that case, I think the searcher will not object to a very simple condition."

"Condition? What condition?" snarled Walters. "I have the lawful right to search him, and I am going to! As for you, I don't know who you are, but you better watch your step, or I will search you, too!"

"I don't think so, ex-sergeant," drawled Blake slowly, watching Walters steadily as the latter regarded him with a faint expression of puzzlement creeping into his eyes.

"Now for the condition," went on Blake.

"I am sure all these other gentlemen will agree that it is perfectly fair. The condition is that before you search your man you shall remove your tunic and hat, and also turn both shirt-sleeves up above the elbow's. In addition, that you shall open each hand wide before beginning the search."

The constable's face went livid.

"Curse you, do you mean to insinuate—"

Blake held up his hand.

"Cut that tone when speaking to me!" he snapped. "I am not accustomed to it, and I do not propose putting up with it. I insinuate nothing. I have stated a very simple condition, which you should be prepared to fulfil. If not, then I think the man you accuse will be perfectly justified in resisting you by force, and there are plenty of witnesses here to prove that he had right on his side."

A murmur of approval greeted Blake's words, and, with another curse, Walters turned aside to throw off his tunic. Bridger shot a look of admiration at Blake, then went on with his stripping. Walters laid his tunic on the bar, and rolled up his shirt-sleeves. Then, in response to a gentle reminder from Blake, he opened his hands wide and held them up for all to see.

As he approached Bridger Blake whispered a few words out of the corner of his mouth to Tinker, and while everyone was engrossed in watching the progress of the search Tinker edged cautiously along towards the spot where Walters' tunic lay.

No one saw the lad's fingers running over the garment in a practised manner that would have done credit to a past-master in the art of pocket-picking. Nor did they see the lad edge back to where Blake stood and whisper a single word to him.

Whatever his faults as a constable may have been, Walters certainly lacked nothing in thoroughness. In his search of Bridger he displayed a passion for care and detail that would have done credit to a less vindictive action; but, search as he would, he had to give up with a baffled shake of the head.

Sexton Blake was wondering all the time if the policeman had really expected to find anything after the conditions which he had laid down, and which Walters had been driven by public opinion to accept. He was inclined to this thought by the word which Tinker had whispered in his ear.

Beyond a surly curse, Walters said nothing as he finished his search and stepped back. Bridger began at once to don his clothes again, but before he had got very far he paused, and gave his attention to what the stranger was saying, as, indeed, was everyone else in the bar, for the stranger was speaking to Walters. The constable had just slipped on his tunic, when Blake said:

"You haven't got them, ex-sergeant."

Walters paused, and looked puzzled. "What do you think you are trying to spring now?" he growled.

"Just what I said," answered Blake pleasantly. "I repeat, ex-sergeant, you haven't got them. You know what I mean!"

For a full half-minute Walters gazed into Blake's eyes; then his right hand went towards the lower corner of the left side of his tunic. Blake nodded ironically:

"That is right, ex-sergeant. That is just what I meant. I said you haven't got them. Nor have you, for here they are —here!" And as he spoke Blake held up his right hand, between the thumb and first finger of which he displayed two uncut diamonds of fairish size. He held them so all the assembled miners could see what they were; then he went on:

"It is not for me to ask whether you are authorised by your superiors to use such methods as you have used here this evening," he said. "But I am inclined to think, from my personal knowledge of the fine body of men to which you belong, that you are not.

"I am not going to say whether it was for this sort of thing you were reduced from the rank of sergeant, but I am going to say that for a constable to enter a public-bar and insist on making a search of a man for illicit diamonds, when at the same time he himself is carrying two uncut stones on his person, is injudicious, to say the least. It might even inspire some persons to draw nasty conclusions, ex-sergeant."

Walters' face was livid, but to save his life he could not speak. His eyes were fixed on Blake's like a bird watching a snake. Later he might explode, and if he did he might be capable of anything; but now —

"Yes, nasty conclusions," went on Blake, in his cold, even tones. "You see, gentlemen, I insisted that the constable should remove his tunic before making his search, for the simple reason that I happen to know of a case where a certain young man —he is on the Breakwater at present —was held up and searched for illicit diamonds.

"He was perfectly innocent, as I now have proof, and soon he will be released. But stones were found on him, nevertheless —for the simple reason that they had been 'planted' either before or during the search. Therefore, as you gentlemen can well understand, he didn't have a chance.

"Understand me, I am not for a moment suggesting that this constable would do such a thing; but I reiterate that, under the circumstances, he should not have been in possession of these rough stones. Just to satisfy myself, I had my young friend search for, find, and abstract the stones while the search was taking place. This is the result. And now I am going to give them back to the constable."

With that Blake strode across to Walters and forced the two diamonds into his hand. The ex-sergeant opened his mouth to speak. His eyes held an ugly look, and Blake knew that the man was on the point of breaking out.

But instead of backing away, Blake bent closer, and whispered so that only Walters heard what was said:

"Take my tip and clear out, ex-Sergeant Walters. Thad Harker is dead, and all his private papers have fallen into my hands. He was shot and killed by Gilbert Harrison on the border of Portuguese East, but before he died he shot and killed Harrison.

"Those papers tell the secret of how a man called Bridger was 'framed' some years ago, and they also tell how some others, including Tom Seagrave, was framed. Your name is in those papers, Walters. Now, get out!"

As Blake drew back, the miners, who had been talking among themselves of the affair, began to murmur, and some voiced audible threats against the constable. It wasn't their threats that made Walters heed Blake's words, for he did not lack physical courage.

It was the cold certainty in Blake's tones, and nothing else, that made him whirl, grab up his revolver, and lurch out into the night, slamming the door after him. When it had closed Blake turned and waved his hand towards the bar.

"Come on, gentlemen," he said pleasantly "the drinks are on me. Name your poison!"

They crowded round him, demanding his name, and when he gave it there was a silence of respect, for not one there had not heard of the famous London criminologist. Then they surged in upon him and Tinker, and it was some minutes before the grateful Jim Bridger could force a way through to his side.

At last he reached Blake, and in a momentary lull said:

"Can we get out of here, Mr. Blake? I must see you in private at once. There is someone else here in the hotel who will be glad to see you, too. We are up against a snag, and if anyone can help us out you are the one."

"I'll come now," responded Blake. "Who is it that wishes to see me?"

"Mademoiselle Yvonne Cartier."

Blake set down his glass, and stared in dumbfounded amazement at Jim Bridger.

"Mademoiselle Yvonne —here!" he gasped. "Good heavens! What on earth has brought her to Speyfontein?"

"My affairs," answered Bridger.

"Lead the way," ordered Blake succinctly.

With that he shouldered his way through the crush, and, followed by Jim Bridger and Tinker, made for the door which led from the bar into the main hall of the hotel.

The Eighth Chapter. Atonement —and Expiation.

IT is little wonder that Blake was amazed at hearing from Jim Bridger of Mademoiselle Yvonne's presence in the hotel at Speyfontein. Not that there was anything remarkable in the fact that she was in South Africa, for Yvonne was an indefatigable globe-trotter, and it would not have been strange to run across her in any out-of-the-way spot.

But it was more than ordinary coincidence to discover that the different purposes which had brought her and Blake to Speyfontein should have come together in a single line leading to one person, namely, Sir Michael Harrison. But if success had crowned Blake's efforts, as much could not be said of Yvonne's.

Guided by Jim Bridger, Blake and Tinker had found Yvonne, Graves, and Margaret Bryan, Yvonne's secretary, seated on the upstairs balcony of the hotel. As it was dusk when Blake and Tinker had ridden in, and as they had entered by the side instead of the front, it is little wonder that neither Yvonne nor Graves saw them.

Nor was Blake more surprised at the news he had received from Bridger than was Yvonne at the sudden entrance of the pair from Baker Street. For a moment she had stared at them incredulously, then she had laughed a little tremulously, coming towards them with both hands outstretched in welcome.

Bridger soon explained how he had met them, and, following that, Blake and Tinker were told the reasons that had brought Yvonne's party to Speyfontein.

Blake had said nothing of his own affairs while he listened, but, in view of the fact that he had found Bridger's name among others in Thad Harker's private papers, and also that Yvonne had mentioned the name of Sir Mike Harrison as the person she was chiefly concerned in unmasking in order to secure justice and a rehabilitated name for Jim Bridger, Blake was putting two and two together and making four as swiftly as his keen mind seized upon and docketed each item of information.

Knowing what he did know of the uses that had been made of Thad Harker in the distant past by Sir Michael Harrison, and the more recent association of Harker and Gilbert Harrison, Blake could read the meaning of a good many things that were still a puzzle to Yvonne.

One thing was clear enough.

This Jim Bridger who had sought Yvonne's assistance could be none other than the same who had been "railroaded" by the Harrisons and Harker to the Breakwater at Cape Town. The papers which Blake had gone through had been sufficiently verbose for Blake to deduce that without even taking the trouble to question Bridger. In fact, those private papers held enough secrets in them to cause considerable sensation in half a dozen quarters if their contents should be divulged.

But on that point Blake had not yet made up his mind. He was pondering this even as Yvonne finished her tale and sat, like the others, waiting for his comments.

"You need look no farther for information of Thad Harker," he said presently. "The man is dead."

"Dead!" cried Bridger, springing to his feet. "What do you mean, Mr. Blake?"

"Just what I say," replied Blake calmly. "Dead —killed —shot."

Then Blake explained briefly why he had come out to South Africa, and how, after his talk with young Tom Seagrave on the Breakwater, he had started out to track down Thad Harker.

From that he went on to describe all that had happened on the frontier of Portuguese East Africa, from the moment when the mysterious shot in the night had driven the book out of his hands until the double murder which had brought the kudu drive to such a dramatic end.

"I didn't find anything of particular interest among the belongings of Gilbert Harrison," he said, in continuation. "But I did find some very interesting and decidedly incriminating papers in Thad Harker's tent. Why the man kept such documents about him I can't imagine, unless it was that he always had in mind the thought that some day they would serve for purposes of blackmail.

"Of course, I am now convinced that this is the reason for the secret rendezvous arranged between him and Gilbert Harrison, for in those papers Harrison was very badly incriminated in several affairs. Not only that, but it is plain from certain things they contain that not only was Gilbert Harrison engaged in many schemes of a shady nature, but he was at the same time realising on securities and using funds belonging to his father, and to which, as his father's manager in South Africa, he had access.

"He must have been very close to the end of his tether when he arrived for that last interview with Harker.

66

"Of course, it is perfectly obvious to me now that the shot which mystified me and Tinker was really intended for Harker. Harrison came there with the desperate intention of killing Harker as the only means of ridding himself of the man's impossible demands.

"That he eventually succeeded we know, but at the same time Harker avenged himself before he died. That is of the past. What we now have to consider is the immediate future.

"It is distinctly interesting to hear from you, Yvonne, that you came out on the same ship with Sir Michael Harrison. I thought it would be necessary for me to take matters up with him in London, and I am glad to know that he is in Speyfontein. I suppose you were able to get little out of him on the voyage out?"

"Not a thing. He was as wary as a wood cock, although I must confess that I used my best efforts."

Blake smiled.

"He must be a hard nut to crack if he resisted your wiles," he remarked.

Yvonne laughed.

"That is the truth, unwilling as I am to confess it."

Blake regarded her quizzically for a few moments, then he changed the subject abruptly.

"Well, in any event, he is the key of the situation now," he said. "A good deal depends on how he takes the news of his son's death. I have reason to believe that he doesn't know of that yet, unless the ex-sergeant, Walters, has told him this evening. But I do not think he has. If I am right in my idea, I think Walters will make for the Portuguese East African border as fast as he can. Before this affair is finished with he will go to the Breakwater on half a dozen counts if he is still in British territory. Therefore, I fancy I shall be the first to break the news to Sir Michael, and I am positive I am the only one who will be able to tell him just how his son died, and why."

"What do you suggest, then?" asked Yvonne.

"I suggest that I send a note to Sir Michael by the Hottentot 'boy' who has been looking after me and Tinker. Toby used to work in the service of Gilbert Harrison, and he will be able to locate his father at once. I shall inform him that I have important news to communicate to him, and I do not think he will refuse to see me. He would be badly advised to do so.

"I think, also, that it would be as well if you came with me,

Yvonne. We can then deal with your case as well, and come to a definite settlement about everything to-night. I haven't the slightest doubt what that will be. I hold too strong a hand for Sir Michael to refuse my demands."

"I shall be glad to go with you." said Yvonne. "It is fortunate for us that you turned up here as you did."

"Do you think, Mr. Blake, that —that you will be able to clear Jim —Mr. Bridger —of everything?" asked Margaret Bryan, looking at Blake through her thick-leased glasses.

"Without the shadow of a doubt," answered Blake kindly. "He has nothing to fear, Miss Bryan. More than that, I can promise that before I finish with our titled friend, Mr. Bridger will receive back all that was taken from him, with full reimbursement for what he has suffered."

"No one can give us back the ten years we have lost," said the girl softly.

"True," responded Blake, who had soon seen how it was between the two after what Yvonne had told him. "No one can give those years back to you, but the years that are to come can be filled with sufficient happiness to make up for them."

"And they will be!" put in Jim Bridger fervently, taking Margaret's hand. "I will make up for them, and we will forget them."

At this point Graves, who had listened with his usual languid manner to the conversation, coughed gently, and the two drew apart in some confusion. Tinker broke the tension by grinning broadly, and with that all laughed. Then, while the others went off to get ready for dinner, Blake and Yvonne strolled to the end of the veranda, where they talked in low, confidential tones until it was time to go down.

After dinner Blake smoked a cigar with Graves while he waited for an answer to the note he had despatched by Toby.

It was nearly ten o'clock before the Hottentot boy returned bearing Sir Michael's answer.

Blake tore it open, and glanced at the contents. It was very brief, and merely said that the writer was working in his private office, and would see Blake there if he would come along. Blake despatched Toby to inform Yvonne that he was waiting, and a few minutes later the two left the hotel and walked down towards the town-hall, opposite which the Harrison offices were situated.

Anyone once having seen Gilbert Harrison would have had no

difficulty in recognising the father as a close blood relation, for the son had been but a younger edition —in appearance —of the older man, although, as Blake knew, he had lacked the deeper cunning of the father.

On entering the building they found themselves in a large general office, at the far end of which was a door partly ajar, and through the opening of which came a gleam of yellow light. A single light only burned in the outer office, which was deserted, and Blake was not sorry that Sir Michael was alone.

The sound of the door closing after them was evidently heard by the magnate, for a moment later the other door swung wide, and they saw his bulky figure silhouetted against the light.

"Is that Mr. Sexton Blake?" he asked, peering towards them.

"Yes, Sir Michael," answered Blake, starting towards him. "I came as soon as I received your note."

The magnate stood aside to allow them to enter, and Blake noticed that he started with surprise at recognising in Blake's companion the same young lady who had travelled out on the ship with him. He made no comment, however, but only bowed and indicated chairs. Then, he seated himself at his desk and regarded Blake speculatively.

"I expected you to come alone, Mr. Blake, since you said you wished to see me on a private matter."

"Mademoiselle Cartier is interested in the same matter, Sir Michael," answered Blake, pleasantly. "Therefore, I thought it best for us to come together."

"What is this matter, Mr. Blake?" asked the magnate, closing and pushing aside the bulky volume which he had been studying. As a matter of fact, Sir Michael Harrison had just been finding out to what extent his son had been defrauding him, and he was not in the mood to discuss any matter, however important it might be, that night.

But Blake's note had had an imperative insinuation which had warned the magnate it would be wiser to find out just why the famous London Criminologist wished to see him.

"First, I have to communicate a piece of news to you that I am afraid will be a considerable shock to you," answered Blake gravely. "May I ask if you have heard from your son within the past few days, Sir Michael?"

The eyes of the magnate hardened.

"My son is up country," he said. "I have not heard from him except a letter he left for me before he went away. What has this to do with your visit, Mr. Blake?"

"Because it falls to my lot to tell you, Sir Michael, that your son was shot and killed on the border of Portuguese East Africa. I am sorry I must appear to state it baldly, but I am simply stating the facts."

In that moment both Blake and Yvonne felt an unwilling admiration for the magnate. His face set like a mask, but not a sign did he give of how the news was affecting him. There was silence for some minutes, then —

"Your news gives me a shock, Mr. Blake," he said slowly. "Did I understand you to say that my son had been shot —shot and killed?"

"Yes."

"When did this happen?"

"A week or more ago."

"Why haven't I been told before?"

"Because my assistant and I were the only white persons who witnessed it, and until I reached Speyfontein this evening I thought you were in England."

"I understand. You —you say that you witnessed this?"

"Yes."

"Then you can tell me who did it?"

"Yes. It was Thad Harker."

That time Sir Michael flinched. His expression told Blake that he was fighting under a tremendous emotion, but was trying not to commit himself to any question that he might regret afterwards. It was that which decided Blake to take a lead and follow it through.

"I had better explain in detail, if you care to hear."

"Please."

"Your son and Thad Harker had a secret rendezvous on the Portuguese border. I and my assistant were there as well, as I was trying to locate Harker in connection with a case I had in hand. I will give you full particulars later, but to-night it is sufficient if I say that your son had strong reasons to fear Harker. He went to the Portuguese border with the intention of killing Harker. He succeeded in doing so."

"Ah! If that is so, then how —"

"I know what you mean. He shot and killed Harker, but before he

70

died Harker was able to draw his revolver and shoot back. Your son died instantaneously, Sir Michael. Following the tragedy, I took over the belongings of each. There was nothing of great moment among those of your son, but I have brought everything back to Speyfontein, Sir Michael, and will turn them over to you.

"Among Harker's belongings I found a large bundle of documents. Those documents were of a very incriminating nature to several persons —several persons, Sir Michael, among the number, I regret to say, was yourself. Those papers are now in my possession, and it is with regard to them that I have come to see you to-night."

Yvonne was sitting with her elbow on the arm of her chair, her chin cupped in her hand, watching Harrison. The latter had his eyes glued on Blake, whose attitude was as cool and restrained as that of a barrister pleading a case of purely academic interest. But, nevertheless, the tenseness in the atmosphere of the room was electric with possibilities, and none knew better than Sexton Blake that now had come the decisive moment.

Would Sir Michael break under the strain of what he feared Blake knew, or would he fight? His words would show.

They came at the end of a full five minutes of what had seemed an eternity of struggling between his will and Blake's. And Yvonne knew in those words, as did Blake, that Blake had won.

"Exactly what do you mean?" he asked.

Blake leant forward, and his voice dropped to a low, hard delivery that could scarcely be heard as far as the door.

He went back twenty years for a beginning, and from that point he unfolded, One by one, the links he had built up from what he had been able to read in the documents he had taken from Thad Harker's tent. It was not a pretty tale he had to tell. It was a story of shame and ruthless cheating, which fell in cold contempt from Blake's lips. Harrison did not interrupt him. Yvonne moved only once —to shift her gaze from Harrison to Blake.

When Blake had finished he leant back. He lifted one hand, and let it fall with a soft thud to his knee.

"That is what I have to say, Sir Michael. It is not the sort of a story one cares to confront a man with when he has reached your years and a position in the world which is where only men of unblemished honour should be.

"Your son killed the man who had been his tool —his tool and yours, and it was the vengeance of Fate that he himself should die by the same hand, even as it was stiffening in death.

"On the Breakwater at Cape Town there are men to-day, sent there by your ruthless greed. At the same hotel where I am staying is a young man whose forehead is disfigured by purple tattoo marks to hide the brand of shame which was put upon him— an innocent man. Those things cannot be permitted to continue. Such things cannot be endured. Justice is tardy, but justice is demanding of you to-night, and you must and will meet those demands."

"I am at your mercy. I —I will do what I can do —to make restitution."

"I am determined on that. I have put down on paper exactly what my demands are. They are heavy —very heavy, but nothing less will satisfy me. I shall leave that paper with you. I shall return here in the morning for your answer. If you refuse, then, I shall place the documents I hold in the hands of the police authorities and allow others to deal with the affair. That is all I have to say to-night."

With that Blake rose and signed to Yvonne. Together they passed out.

•　　•　　•　　•　　•

The following morning Blake was wakened early by Tinker.

"Sir Michael shot himself in his office last night, guv'nor. I have just come from there. I managed to get inside, and the police want to get in touch with you. There is a big thick envelope addressed to you. They found it on his desk."

Blake dressed hurriedly, and, on descending to the ground floor found a sergeant of police asking for him. They went into a private sitting-room, where the sergeant handed Blake the document of which Tinker had spoken. Blake opened it.

In a few minutes he saw that the chief document was a full and complete confession by Sir Michael, and, accompanying it were detailed papers covering all the demands Blake had made. There was, in addition, a will in which he split up his remaining estate among several charities in atonement for the past. When he had finished, Blake laid the papers down and turned to the sergeant.

"I presume you want my statement, sergeant?" he said.

"If you please, Mr. Blake."

"I will go along with you and give it to you. It will take a considerable time. I hope it will not be necessary to make all the details public, for, if he sinned, Sir Michael has atoned —he has atoned and made restitution. Let us go!"

Sir Michael had indeed made restitution.

Blake, Yvonne, and the others remained in Speyfontein for another week to attend to the necessary formalities, but at the end of that time they started for Cape Town.

Jim Bridger had received back the diamond mine which he had been tricked out of, together with the equivalent of what it had produced during the past ten years.

He had begged that Margaret should remain in South Africa and marry him at once, but, even though Yvonne consented, Margaret would not hear of it. She was determined to return with Yvonne and continue her work until Yvonne was able to replace her. Blake's representations soon secured the release of young Tom Seagrave, and five more men received pardons and reimbursement, although they never knew that it was due to Sexton Blake.

Certain facts inevitably crept out, but the whole of the truth remained a secret among just a few persons, which was as Blake would have it considering that Sir Michael had paid the penalty after acting as his own judge.

And, six months later, Jim Bridger was glad that Margaret had been so firm for, through Blake, he was placed in the hands of a clever surgeon who, after removing the tattoo marks, placed him under treatment of ultra-violet rays, with the result that, at the end of that time, almost every vestige had vanished of the brand of the I.D.B.

THE END.
[27200 WORDS]

The U. J. Detective Supplement.
Scotland Yard's "Foreign Squad."

It is not only in his native country that the British policeman labours.

Although it is not generally known, Scotland Yard maintains a special squad of detectives in many Continental ports whose duties are varied and many.

Why they are there and what they do is described in the following article.

STRANGE as it may sound, there are numbers of English policemen, all of whom are on the strength at Scotland Yard, doing duty in foreign ports.

These men form part of a special squad, and their duties are peculiar.

They are in constant touch with Scotland Yard as well as the police force of the country in which they are temporarily on duty—a duty which is twofold. To keep an eye on all persons landing at the port to which they are attached, to advise the local police of the arrival of suspicious English crooks, and to notify Scotland Yard of the departure of foreign criminals and suspects who embark for England.

Such squads consist of a detective-inspector, two or more detective-sergeants, and perhaps four or more ordinary detectives.

All of them must speak the language of the country in which they are stationed, a point of the first consideration when they are being selected. The second is an intimate knowledge of English and Continental lags, smugglers, racecourse thieves, and gamblers who make a practice of trying to entrap the unwary into games of cards either on the trip to or from an English port.

Travellers to France, for example, would possibly fail to notice a couple of men in plain clothes who stand unobtrusively near the gangway as the passengers are disembarking from the cross-Channel steamers at Boulogne, Calais, or Dieppe.

Passengers pass on their way to the Customs sheds, where their baggage is examined and passports scrutinised, all unaware of the ferret-like glances of these two apparently casual loungers.

Suddenly a man, too smartly dressed to be a gentleman, of

somewhat horsey appearance, is about to step jauntily off the gangway, when a hand reaches out and taps him on the shoulder.

With a well-feigned start of surprise, the man turns round, and a momentary flicker of recognition lights up his face.

"This way, Jemmy! I want you a minute!" says the hitherto unconcerned lounger. And the traveller, without another word, follows his unexpected host into the police-office.

"What's the game?" inquires the officer.

"Races!" laconically replies Jemmy.

"Well, you had better mind your P's and Q's. We had several complaints from Longchamps last week," rejoins the officer.

Jemmy walks away, cursing his luck but hoping for the best.

Later that day comes a telephone-message through from the Paris police to the effect that a well-known English racing-man had been robbed while attending the race for the Grand Prix of French and English banknotes. The description of the man tallies with that of Jemmy, and this fact is phoned to all the French Channel ports.

Next day, Jemmy, who has reached France by way of Calais, thinks he would prefer to return home by way of Boulogne, and having got rid of his "swag" in Paris by arrangement with one of the shady frequenters of a well-known crooks' resort, makes his way to Boulogne with the return half of the ticket of a pal who has gone out that way.

Jemmy's exploit has preceded him, and as he walks along the quay he is pulled up by a confrere of the Calais officer and handed over to the custody of the gendarmes.

Not long since a noted saccharine-smuggler, a man in a large way of business, was known by the French police to be preparing for a trip to England. The special squad was informed, and directly the man stepped on board the Channel steamer his departure was flashed across to Dover, where he was promptly arrested. Five hundred ounces of the commodity were found concealed in his clothing.

Sometimes the "wanted" men put up a fierce fight, and life is risked as well as limb.

Two years ago a well-known Continental bank-thief made a desperate and determined effort to rob the Bank of France. He actually succeeded in snatching a bundle of fifty thousand franc-notes from the counter, and managed to get into a waiting motor-car, and, so far, make good his escape. His description had been given to the police, who, in turn, with all possible dispatch, warned the police at all the cross-Channel ports.

As the thief, muffled up to look like a confirmed invalid, stepped on the gangway just as it was being drawn ashore, a sergeant of the special squad sprang after him. A desperate struggle ensued, while the men in charge of the gangway, uncertain whether to push it back towards the deck or the already receding quay, held it suspended in mid-air.

Fiercely the two men fought for the space of a minute or so, first one and then the other seeming to get the upper-hand.

All the while the two slipped lower and lower down the gangway towards the sea, while the steamer's captain, uncertain with whom he had to deal, edged his boat slowly out into the Channel.

The arrival of another member of the squad recalled the men in charge of the gangway to their senses, and the stage was drawn slowly back to land, just as the frantic efforts of the escaping thief had drawn both men to the extreme end of it.

A minute later and both would have been struggling in the sea some twenty feet below the level of the quay, a position from which it is doubtful whether either would have been rescued alive had the desperate thief been able to maintain his hold.

There was no doubt, from what the thief afterwards stated, that if both of them had reached the water it was his intention to have drowned his captor even at the risk of his own life for having pierced his disguise.

It is not only for the purpose of watching for the arrival and departure of known criminals from Continental ports to this country, and vice versa, that English policemen are called abroad. A number of British policemen are frequently to be found in the United States. But in this instance they can hardly be said to come under the heading of the "Foreign Squad." They are there for the purpose of studying methods of traffic control as practised in the great American cities. Several American ideas in this direction have been adopted in this country, and several of our ideas have been imported into America.

There are, of course, occasions when men from Scotland Yard travel abroad to bring back in custody a person who has broken bail and fled the country, or a person who has fled in anticipation of arrest for some crime or another. But this is nothing to do with the "Foreign Squad." This work usually comes under the department dealing with extradition, and is an entirely different branch of the Yard's activities, which will be dealt with more fully in a subsequent article.

Criminals of all classes pass through the hands of these "Special Guardians" of our shores, and many are stopped before they can set foot on these shores.

By exercise of the same amount of vigilance on this side we help to control the movements of Continental thieves who are on their way abroad and so warn the police of other countries of the coming visit of undesirables.

STINIE MORRISON in the dock. When called upon to plead before the magistrate he exclaimed dramatically, " if I were standing before Almighty God, I could give but one answer — I am not guilty ! " "*Daily Mirror.*"

BEFORE THE EVENT
No. 4.-STINIE MORRISON.
By FREDERIC A. FELTON

This is the fourth article of a brilliant series dealing with men our contributor has known before the event which brought them to the dock on the capital charge. Stinie Morrison, a veritable King of the Underworld, is the most fascinating and perhaps the most famous of them all. Many details of his life before the deed which sent him to penal servitude are here revealed for the first time.

LEON BERON, whose body was found on Clapham Common with the letter "S" cut in each cheek.
"*Daily Mirror.*"

ROUND the blazing fire of a certain little-known club of which I am a member, I am sometimes induced to regale guests from the provinces with stories of the great criminals I have met during my lengthy career as a journalist, who has made a speciality of crime writing.

At these select gatherings I try to take my hearers behind the scenes, to reveal secrets concerning the crook under discussion which will make them think, and to tell what we journalists call "the story behind the story," that is to say, the story of the crime which has not been made public, but which has come into my possession during and after the investigation by the police.

And I find that among narratives concerning murderers with whom I have been professionally, and in some cases privately, associated that of Stinie Morrison occupies a foremost position in holding the attention of my hearers.

But was Stinie Morrison a murderer? The law has answered the question in the affirmative; for Morrison was found guilty of the murder of Leon Beron on Clapham Common, and sentenced to death.

This sentence was afterwards commuted to penal servitude for life, and Morrison died in Parkhurst prison over a year ago.

Legally, as I have said, Stinie Morrison was guilty. But there are still many eminent criminologists, lawyers, and even detectives who believe that Morrison's was not the hand which struck the fatal blow, although they are inclined to agree that he was well aware of the identity of the guilty man, and, for reasons he never revealed even to his closest friend, was desirous of shielding the culprit.

Let me tell the amazing story of mystery and intrigue, however, so that my readers can form their own independent opinion.

Journalistic business first brought me into contact with Stinie Morrison. This was some seven or eight months before he stood in the dock at the grim Old Bailey charged with the murder of Beron.

At that time a great deal of rumour was spreading concerning the terrible things which went on among the crooks of the East End. I was sent to find out the truth and tell it to the world.

For six weeks I lived in the seething underworld which lies east of Aldgate pump.

I slept by day and went out by night, when the denizens of this mystic area emerge from their lairs to make war upon their fellows and plot and plan against Society generally.

I dressed the part, lived the part, and met scores of weird men and women, some bad, some good, but many of whom remain my acquaintances to this day.

In stifling night clubs reeking with vodka, that potent Russian drink which makes men into demons, in gambling hells, in revolutionary gatherings and in the known haunts of men who could be induced to "out" an enemy with a sandbag for five shillings or murder him for £10 I spent night after night.

And when my task was over and I rushed to the seaside, the breezes which blew on me from the sea at Brighton were like unto the breath of Heaven.

The articles I was enabled to write as the result of my stay in the East End, often in danger, and constantly running the risk of being flung into the street, created a great sensation up and down the country.

For the first time, I think, I told people the plain, unvarnished truth about the great game of life as it is played by the men and women of the underworld of the East End.

And the man who gave me the most valuable assistance I received anywhere in compiling my articles was Stinie Morrison!

I was introduced to him by a prison warder friend through whose hands Morrison had passed. The two were good friends, and the mere facts that the warder vouched for my discretion was enough for Stinie.

I played the straight bat with him, and, although he was a crook who subsequently turned out to be a murderer as well, I am bound to say he played it with me.

He took me practically everywhere I wanted to go. He piloted me into opium dens, gambling hells, secret society meetings, clubs, dance halls, protected me when I was in danger through any little indiscretion in conversation, and, generally, acted as my guide, philosopher and friend.

Morrison was an extraordinary character. By calling he was a baker. But he was a crook as well, and spent ten times the money he earned as a baker in having a good time. This money of course, he got from tainted sources.

There were three physical characteristics about Stinie Morrison which stood out clear and distinct. In the first place he had a face like a Greek god.

Secondly he had piercing magnetic eyes which at times were slumberous pools, but at others became pin-points of livid flame.

Those eyes would have arrested attention anywhere. Thirdly, he had beautifully shaped hands, long white tapering fingers, always well kept, but hands possessing the strength of steel.

Added to this Morrison had a fascinating, compelling manner, especially with women, and, although by reason of his foreign parentage he wrote ungrammatically, he spoke well and interestingly.

Morrison himself told me that he was born in Sydney, New South Wales, but while still an infant he left for Russia with his parents, who were Russian Jews.

He added that he had lived in Russia and France for extended periods and had come to London in 1900.

In the East End, to which he migrated as naturally as a duck takes to water, Morrison met many kindred spirits.

When I made his acquaintance and, night after night, went about in his company, he proved unmistakably to me that in that mystic region where night is turned into day he wielded certain power which none disputed.

With an imperious gesture of his hand he could, and did in my presence, quell an angry outburst. He was a fine boxer, wrestler, and swordsman, and he played well on the flute.

A cooler gambler I have never seen. He was an expert at poker, and whatever hand he held, whether good or simply a "bluffing" hand, his face was granite-like, and never gave his opponents the slightest clue as to the cards he held.

His mastery over his facial muscles was supreme, and I have seen him face a knife or a revolver in the reeking atmosphere of an East End vice-haunt without flickering an eyelid.

Such was the man and the murderer as I knew him. It has been stated over and over again that Stinie Morrison was a close associate of the notorious Peter the Painter who figured so largely in the historic siege of Sydney Street, which was fully described in these pages some months ago.

Personally I do not believe it. The two may have been acquainted, but I have the best of reasons for stating that the twain were never associated in any criminal enterprises. They were crooks of a totally different calibre.

Now for the thrilling story of the crime.

Rather early in the morning on the first day of January, 1911, my telephone bell rang, and, I was instructed to proceed at once to a pond at Clapham Common.

Here had been found the body of one Leon Beron. He had been killed by many blows on the head with a jemmy or some similar weapon, and on his face were cuts made by a sharp instrument, after death.

So commenced my association with the mysterious affair which subsequently became known as the Crime of the Scarlet "S."

For the knife marks on the dead man's face bore a strong resemblance to the letter I have mentioned. And first theories jumped in the direction that the scarlet S signified the word SPY.

Beron was a Russian Jew, a man who lived well although he had no visible means of income. And, as I say, the first assumption was that he was a spy and that "S" stood for the Yiddish spik (spy), the French (spion), or the German schlucher, which means traitor.

Beron lived, as a matter of fact, on the rents of nine houses which he owned, and it was a general belief that he carried about with him always sums of between £20 and £30 in gold, and wore a gold watch and chain worth from £30 to £40.

When the dead body was examined by the police, the watch and chain were missing.

So bristling was the crime with baffling elements that the police got their teeth into it like terriers. In eight days they arrested

Morrison, who was also known as Morris Stein.

He was apprehended by Mr. Wensley, now one of the famous "Big Four" of Scotland Yard, and the late Chief Inspector Ward.

The theory of the prosecution was that Morrison had lured Beron from Whitechapel, where they were known to have been together, to Clapham for the sake of his money and jewellery.

Morrison vehemently protested his innocence, and when called upon to plead before the magistrate when charged he exclaimed dramatically, "If I were standing before Almighty God, I could give but one answer —I am not guilty."

Throughout the whole of his life Morrison had a sense of the dramatic. He dearly loved to play to the gallery, a fact that probably arose because at one period of his chequered career he was an actor.

In my visits to him in the East End, I found the same love of the dramatic as he showed through his trial, showed even until the day when his eyes closed in death.

The police followed up clue after clue with tireless persistence. They proved that at the time Morrison left home on the night prior to the crime, he had no money in his possession.

Yet when he returned to his lodgings, on January 3rd, he threw gold on the table, and took off his clothes which were bloodstained, and asked his landlady to burn them.

Then the police added another damning link to the chain of evidence. They found that Morrison had sold the gold watch belonging to the dead man.

Finally we reached the court at the Old Bailey before Mr. Justice Darling. The investigation of the case lasted nine full days and was, I well recollect, marked by a series of startling and dramatic incidents.

The most remarkable of these incidents, and one which, in the view of several eminent legal authorities to whom I spoke, was unique, occurred on the last day, when Counsel for the Crown was in the middle of his concluding comments on the evidence.

Throughout the trial, controversy had raged round the point whether (as the police swore) Morrison had suggested that he was accused of murder before any charge of that character had been made against him or whether, as he contended was the case, he was told on his arrival of the nature of the accusation.

At the dramatic eleventh hour, a police constable named Greaves came forward, and gave evidence that within a few minutes of

Morrison being taken to the police station, a sergeant told him that the charge against him would be one of wilful murder.

This direct contradiction by a police constable of the statements which had been sworn to by other and superior officers was subsequently the subject of a searching inquiry by Viscount Cave, the present Lord Chancellor, who expressed himself satisfied that Greaves' version of the matter was incorrect.

After they had consulted for half an hour, the jury returned into Court with a verdict of Guilty, and he was sentenced to death.

Morrison, dramatist to the last, electrified the dense crowd in Court by an outburst as Mr. Justice Darling concluded the sentence of death with the words, "And may the Lord have mercy on your soul."

"I decline such mercy," shrieked Morrison, "and I don't believe there is a God in Heaven, either."

After the sentence, there sprang up in Morrison's favour a great wave of public feeling. Despite the verdict of the jury and the inevitable passing of the death sentence, there were many persons who still entertained doubts as to whether the right man had been convicted.

No fewer than 70,000 people signed a petition for his reprieve, and strong appeals were made to the Attorney-General.

These prayers of the people had the desired effect, and in due course Morrison's sentence was commuted to one of penal servitude for life.

Morrison was at first taken to Dartmoor, and, at Waterloo, he had a violent struggle with the warders who were in charge of him.

At the prison he smashed all the movable articles in his cell, and had to be put in a strait-jacket.

When he had recovered and, indeed, till the end of his life, he protested his innocence; and it is interesting to note that ere he had been in prison a year, 40,000 additional people had signed another petition praying for his release.

Even now I have by no means exhausted the list of thrills and sensations which marked the charge against the man who had been so useful and courteous to me during my memorable experience in the dark East End.

The whole case was remarkable for the nature of the evidence. One girl who said she saw Morrison wearing a £5 piece on his watch-chain (a similar coin to one alleged to have been stolen from the murdered man) later said her evidence was not true.

Another of the witnesses attempted suicide.

Morrison's bearing in the dock captured sympathy. Tall, physically strong and well built, with a mass of black hair, brilliant in passion and winning in repose, he took a vivid interest in his trial, ejaculating questions and advising his counsel.

When he was sentenced, his face blanched. He went livid with passion. At that moment he looked the murderer, whereas a few minutes before he had looked a fine upstanding young man of fine qualities.

I have known many men who led double lives; Stinie Morrison had a double nature.

From prison he wrote many affectionate letters to a young woman living not far from the Elephant and Castle, with whom he was undoubtedly very much in love. In these he again and again declared his innocence. One poignant sentence from a letter I was permitted to see ran:

"Believe me innocent, darling, no matter how strong the evidence might be against me. For I take the Almighty to witness my innocence. God grant me my liberty once more, sweetheart, and — well, wait and see, my darling."

In another letter to the same girl, which I was also permitted to see, came the sentence:

"I am quite well, dearest. I eat well and sleep well, knowing nothing of the crime alleged against me. It is difficult to believe that I could have been found guilty."

On one occasion after his sentence, but before his reprieve, Mr. Abinger, who made such a brilliant fight for the defence, went to see his client. The well-known counsel afterwards gave me his own account of the visit.

"I went to see Morrison," said Mr. Abinger, "to ask him to sign a petition. Immediately he replied, 'I absolutely refuse to sign. I did not do the murder, and I am not going to pray for mercy.'

"I was greatly affected, but he steadfastly refused. At last I said to him, 'Cannot you tell me anything which will assist?' He replied, 'Well, yes. A short time before the murder I forged a cheque for £200 drawn on the London and South Western Bank.

"'I was paid in banknotes. I took the notes to Cook's, in Ludgate Circus, and converted them into French money, then I took a 'bus to

Cook's, in Piccadilly, reconverting the French banknotes into English money. I did this to render it difficult to trace the notes to me.'

"'But why,' I said, 'did you not tell this to your solicitors before; it is of the greatest importance."'

"He replied, 'I thought you would get me off on the charge of murder, and it meant pleading Guilty to a charge of forgery and serving a sentence of penal servitude. You can see, sir, I was in no want of money at all.'

"Immediately," continued the famous defender, "I placed the facts before Morrison's solicitor, and they were quickly verified by the bank and by Messrs. Cook's.

"I then got on the telephone and was fortunate enough to find the Home Secretary, Mr. Winston Churchill, at the end of the wire.

"I told him the story quickly, and he asked me to go at once to the Home Office and repeat it. I was afterwards informed that it was found accurate in every particular.

"The next day I received a wire from the secretary of State informing me he had reprieved Stinie Morrison. The public were never told the reason for the reprieve, and there was much speculation about it."

Some six months later another statement in favour of Morrison, which had been kept dark owing to the fear its possessor had of her husband, was revealed to Mr. Abinger in his chambers in the Temple, London.

On the face of this, another petition (the second I have already mentioned) was presented to the Home Office asking for the convict's immediate release. But this was refused, and Morrison was removed from Dartmoor to Parkhurst.

In all, he served about ten years. Shortly after his arrival at Parkhurst, which was in 1912, Morrison began voluntarily to abstain from food, complaining that he could not eat it.

He had spells of abstention and then became better and went out of hospital. Finally he became run down again and was placed under mental observation. His diet was changed, and he ate some food for about ten days.

Then he refused to eat anything, but he gave no hint that he was abstaining from food with a view to destroying himself.

Just before his death Morrison had to be fed from a feeding-cup. Yet, when normal, he had an enormous appetite.

From time to time Morrison was questioned by the prison Medical Officer as to why he would not take food. The reply was typical of the man. He declared that other prisoners serving long sentences had had their cases reconsidered, but he could not secure the same concession.

I am afraid that as the end drew near Stinie Morrison's mind gave way. One of the strange things he did was to put both his jam and his pudding into his tea, of which he drank two pints daily.

When he was threatened with forcible feeding he became very violent in spite of his weakened condition, and threatened to smash the windows and cut his throat. He gave more trouble than ninety out of every hundred prisoners who go to Parkhurst.

Yet at the back of Morrison's brain, affected as it might have been, I myself convinced there was a cunning scheme. His idea was to force the hands of the authorities by refusing nourishment.

When his eyes closed in death, his troublous and storm-tossed life over, his great frame was not emaciated. His death was caused by heart failure and debility, aggravated by voluntarily abstaining from food. Such was the verdict of the jury.

And Morrison's remains were enclosed in a black-painted coffin and taken from Parkhurst prison to the parish cemetery at Carisbrooke, Isle of Wight. He was thirty-nine years of age.

This then is the true story of Stinie Morrison, told in its entirety, perhaps, for the first time. A few hours before I sat down to write it I passed the house where he took refuge for a time in the York Road, Lambeth. And, as I passed, I wondered yet once more if when I met Stinie Morrison under the circumstances I have described I really met a murderer.

And I am afraid I am still wondering.

Great Escapes.

By H. V. Tovey.

No. 4—THE MAN IN THE PACKING-CASE.

By H. V. TOVEY,

The big packing-case split open, and a curious sailor, looking inside, called out in horrified tones : " Look, there is a man here ! "

That men will frequently risk their lives to regain lost freedom is well known. But the subject of the following article risked his life for the sole purpose of being able to risk it again in battle. His scheme for escape all but won through, and was only detected at the eleventh hour by an unforeseen accident.

MEN have been known to risk their lives for anything—or nothing. For money —the love of a woman—for the risk of notoriety —for the excitement and the risk itself. But it has seldom happened that a man has risked his life for the sake of having the opportunity of losing it in battle afterwards.

To run this risk by travelling some two hundred miles in a packing-case as "luggage" by railway, with the certainty of a shortage of air to breathe and no food but a bunch of bananas, and a little wine-and-water in a bottle, is a feat that would cause most men to pause and think before undertaking such a formidable task.

Yet this was the feat undertaken by Lieutenant Otto Kahn in the December of 1914, although, as his record shows, this was by no means his first attempt to escape from the custody of his captors and regain his own country.

Scene 1 of this comedy-drama was laid at Dorchester, a place which twice before in our island history has afforded a camping-ground for our alien enemies. Scene 2 was enacted at Gravesend, when only a short distance separated him from the waters of the sea and freedom.

About 55 B.C., Julius Caesar's legions camped at Dorchester during their invasion of Britain, and part of the mounds then raised by them for defence still remain as witness of their energy and military skill, for these earth ramparts command the approaches to their camp as well to-day as then.

New Uses for an old Camp.

Still later the old camp was made the scene of the internment of French prisoners taken during the Napoleonic wars. And during the world war it was adopted once more as an internment camp for German prisoners.

It would seem that our earliest visitors found the place much to their liking, for they stayed there long enough to build what was, in those days, a mighty Roman camp. Those who came after had a camp built for them, and liked it so little that they were for ever planning to escape.

When the internment of every alien enemy was found necessary in the late autumn of 1914, on account of the prevalence of spying and the astounding ease with which news of vital importance to the enemy found its way out of this country, a large camp was built just outside Dorchester, on the site of the old Roman encampment. In this a large number of enemy aliens who were beyond military age were interned.

The place was wired round with barbed wire, charged at night with a very powerful electric current. Enormous arc-lights turned night into day, so that with these precautions and a strong armed guard always on duty, there seemed little chance of escape.

As time went on, and prisoners of war began to come in, it was thought advisable to send some of the older internees home, so making more room for newcomers, while saving our own food, and putting the job of keeping these "useless" men on the shoulders of the Germans.

Amongst the first batch of prisoners of war sent to Dorchester was Lieutenant Otto Kahn, a typical Prussian officer, tall —for he stood over six feet —spare of build, fairhaired, and blue-eyed, with all the swagger and assurance of men of his type.

He was in America at the outbreak of hostilities, and started for home on the s.s. Potsdam. Luck was against him, for the Potsdam fell a victim to a British light cruiser, and, without a show of fight, hauled down her colours. The vessel was taken, a prize of war, into Falmouth, and Kahn, with other Germans, was sent to Dorchester.

A Plan of Escape.

What follows is based on Kahn's story, as told after his recapture.

So far as accommodation and privileges went, the English internment camps were Elysium compared to those in Germany in which British prisoners were condemned to live.

Prisoners who would give their parole were allowed to go into Dorchester and spend money (of which they seemed to have abundance) as they liked. They were allowed to buy tools with which to exercise a taste in carpentering and so forth, as well as luxuries in the way of food, wines, and other things which British people were already learning to do without.

Some had made articles of furniture, veritable works of art, and when the order, come for their deportation each prisoner was allowed a certain quantity of space for personal belongings to be taken with him on the journey home.

As soon as it became known that a number of the prisoners were to go, Kahn tried, after consultation with the others, to formulate some plan by which he was to escape from Dorchester and journey with the others to Germany by way of Holland.

Long councils of war were held after the prisoners had been shut in for the night, and the possibility of the adoption of a disguise, the impersonation of another deportee, and other means, were considered at length.

All of these were finally turned down, for though the authorities were easy to the verge of laxity in their treatment of the prisoners, it was not thought they would be lax enough to allow anyone to slip through their fingers by any of these simple methods.

Swedish Matches.

Finally, Kahn hit upon a plan which all thought might meet with success. It seemed simple, and one not likely to lead to suspicion. And the risk, such as there was, was Kahn's, and Kahn's alone.

A number of large packing-cases had been secured from the town in which the deportees were to pack their belongings. Kahn, through a fellow-conspirator who was going to Germany, had managed to get possession of a large case which had once contained Swedish matches.

It had a large stencilled mark on the lid: "Non-poisonous. Safety Matches," enclosed in a diamond, innocent enough in appearance to have passed without notice.

This case was strengthened on the inside to enable it to carry the weight of a man, and was fitted with every possible convenience that thought could devise.

There were arm and leg rests —strips of webbing nailed to the sides of the case, so that the inmate could secure himself against being tossed about and bruised by any rough handling the case might be subjected to on the journey, a pad was fitted for the head, and everything done that was possible to make life endurable in such a confined space.

Such exceeding care was taken to make the inside of the case invisible from the outside that it as nearly as possible defeated the aim of the conspirators —to get Kahn out alive —by making the case so airtight that he was nearly suffocated. No doubt he would have been quite, but for the accident which saved his life and deprived him of liberty until the end of the war.

The plan was to put Kahn in this case, fasten down the lid, and label it as belonging to one of the other deportees.

In the Case.

This was done the last thing, and the case was placed on a motor lorry in the camp with the belongings of the other prisoners and taken to the railway.

Kahn had answered the roll call after breakfast as usual, and then went to his room ostensibly to read.

Instead, he was packed in his case with some bananas and a bottle of wine and some brandy, the lid being fastened securely down.

In due course the case was removed with other luggage. Much to the consternation of those in the plot, it had a lot of other cases and bundles heaped on top of it, as, owing to its size, it was put at the bottom of the heap.

At the railway station, which was reached without mishap, the plotters received another damper to their hopes. Instead of travelling by the ordinary service they and their belongings were put in a special train and sent a long way round the country, to avoid taking them and their packages out of the train again and transferring them to another, in addition to the added risk and trouble of having to transport them all across London from Paddington to Fenchurch Street, on the road for Tilbury.

Practically a whole day was taken up in this way, Kahn sweating and almost suffocated by the lack of air and the heat engendered by the mass of packages lumped on top of his living tomb.

Release—Just let Time.

This part of the story is taken from Kahn's own words, given to the police after he had been discovered.

"After some hours of this hellish confinement," he added, "I lost consciousness, and all I remember is that after what seemed to me to be days I was bumped down, I could feel my 'coffin' being handled, and then I must have gone off again, as I can remember no more till there was a terrific bump, and I could fed fresh air blowing on my face,"

What did actually happen is best told by others who had the handling of the deportees and their luggage when the train reached Tilbury, where they were detrained for embarkation on the s.s. Batavier for Hamburg.

Some railway men were told off to take the luggage down to a tender which was lying just inside the stupendous wooden barrier which had been erected across the river from Tilbury to Gravesend, a barrier of sufficient strength to have resisted the attacks of torpedo boats if ever the German fleet had ventured as far up the river mouth.

Needless to say the baggage did not receive careful treatment, and once the human cargo had been put on board, the packages followed as fast as hands could throw them, regardless of size or value.

In spite of the frantic protests of those in the grim secret, the case of "Safety Matches" was clumsily bundled end over end to the deck, landing on one end with a shivering crash.

It split open and a curious sailor, looking inside, called out in horrified tones: "Look! There's a man in here."

The Alarm Goes Back.

Others, attracted by these words, flocked round the case, the remainder of the top cover was ripped off, and when the captain of the tender arrived there was revealed the seemingly dead body of a tall young man whose hands and feet were held in loops to the sides of the case.

His head was cut and bleeding, while his face was bruised and discoloured as evidence of the rough handling the case had been subjected to while getting it on the tender.

Both the police and the military were called, and a message sent through to Dorchester revealed the fact that a prisoner, Otto Kahn, had been missing since early morning without the authorities having been able to find any trace of his whereabouts.

Kahn was taken out of the case by the authorities, and it took some hours of medical treatment to bring him round to consciousness.

Later, the remainder of the plot was revealed. It was that once the Batavier had got outside Territorial waters the case was to have been opened and Kahn set at liberty, to the delight of the Dutch and the mortification of the English seamen on board. Unfortunately for their plan the case was opened too soon, and in a way never intended by the conspirators.

After he had recovered consciousness Kahn was placed in a cell at Gravesend Police Station, and, later taken back to Dorchester, where he was tried for breaking his parole and sent to undergo a term of imprisonment at a place where breaking out was not so easy, and privileges were few.

A Previous Attempt.

It appeared on inquiry that this was not Kahn's only effort to regain his freedom. He spoke English perfectly, and on one occasion almost talked himself into liberty.

He ordered himself a golf suit, and by his apparent command of military matters nearly managed to get free from Dorchester by engaging a cabman to drive him to a well known country seat near, where it was public property that there was a private Links.

When recaptured, owing to the astuteness of the cabby, Kahn was found to have a large sum of English gold in his possession, sufficient to have enabled him to get to London, where he was to have joined a friend.

They were to have made their way to the Docks in the hope of being able to bribe some seamen to give them passage to Holland, Spain, or some other neutral place.

Kahn's English, although nearly perfect, was the cause of his undoing. He asked the cabman to tell him where he could get a certain brand of cigarettes, asking for "Abdewlla."[1] The cabby took him to a shop, and the shop-keeper telephoned for the police.

How these men managed to communicate with each other was a mystery, but Kahn had got into communication with another prisoner at Donington Hall, and the two had arranged to meet in London.

The other man did reach there, and was actually in London at the time of one of the Zeppelin raids on the East End. He was in hiding, dressed as a clergyman, and during the raid actually came into the streets and helped the police to dress some of those wounded by German bombs.

He was on the scene at the time a well-known public house was destroyed by another bomb, and, somehow managed to get into the hands of the police, escaping because the street lights went out at a critical moment. He was afterwards arrested at the Docks, when he had almost completed his arrangements for getting away, but Nemesis, in the shape of a German idiom helping to put the keeper of a little hotel, where he had put up, on his track by his having adopted the German custom of writing his supposed address as "William Smith, Hight St., No. 125, Leeds." This un-English method of writing his address betrayed him.

It was not till after the Armistice that he went home.

---

[1] This is Abdulla cigarettes. /drf

ABDULLA

"To smoke an Abdulla 75 is to become conscious of a new pleasure added to life. This exceptional Virginia Cigarette has the hall-mark of purity and charm which has so long distin-guished Abdulla Turkish and Egyptian."

25 for 1/11

VIRGINIA

No 75

Laughter In Court!

Charged with being drunk, a man who had given the name of Dick Whittington was stated to be addicted to the use of methylated spirits.

Magistrate: "Dick Whittington up-to-date!"

A woman having taken the oath, kissed the hand of the court usher instead of the Testament. She blushed and apologised.

The usher: "Oh, don't mention it!"

Having used the Yiddish word "shemozzle," a policeman was asked what the word meant. He replied readily:

"A shemozzle means a row in which more than six people are engaged."

"He was in a collapsible state," said a constable, describing the condition of a man who had got the worst of a street-fight.

"If my husband was a fool —which he isn't —he'd tell me what he earns. I don't suppose you tell your missus," said a woman to a magistrate.

Magistrate (regretfully): "My wife has only to look in 'Whitaker' to find out for herself."

A complainant said that her young woman lodger cooked kippers, etc., on an oil-stove in the bath.

Magistrate: "I've heard of it being used as a coal-cellar before, but not as a kitchen!"

Asked where a prisoner was, a gaoler replied:

"He's been taken to the infirmary in a 'venomous' condition!"

"I saw him pass the remark," said a constable, speaking of a prisoner.

"Then your eye must photograph sound!" retorted the magistrate.

Solicitor to defendant in a rent case: "Have you the use of the scullery?"

Defendant: "The use of it? I should say! I sleep in it!"

"Why can't you work?" asked the magistrate of a man.

"I've got 'pneumatics' in my arm," replied the man in a confidential whisper.

Humanity in Blue

The London Policeman, despite his association with crime and criminals, still remains an intensely human man at heart.

OLD people and children, especially the latter, have the most correct appreciation of policemen of all the inhabitants of this country. Naturally enough, the criminal classes regard him with suspicion not unmixed with aversion; but the one outstanding fact about the whole force is that the men composing it are, above all, intensely human.

Some years ago a prominent Academician set all London talking by a picture he exhibited at the Royal Academy. It was one of a policeman, with arm outstretched, holding up the traffic at Piccadilly Circus, while a nurse pushed a perambulator containing a baby across the roadway, with hundreds of vehicles of all kinds waiting for "His Majesty the Baby" to pass.

No specially-designed tableau could have told in so forcible a manner the story of "Robert's" weakness for the young and helpless.

Take that busiest of spots, the crossings by the Mansion House, and see with what care a City constable will pilot a blind or infirm person across the never-ceasing stream of traffic, leaving them safe, with a smile and a nod, never expecting or receiving more than a heartily extended "Thanks!"; all, in most cases, that the poor traveller has to give.

These little human acts are of every day occurrence, and are to be witnessed by one and all. There are many others done unseen, and it is of these I will tell.

A wretched home in the slums; no fire, no food. A woman and three or four children huddling together for warmth, all eating greedily at small portions of bread, while a man, obviously the father, stands gloomily near the door, listening apprehensively to the slightest sound from outside.

It comes at last. A stern, commanding knock, and the door is opened to admit a policeman, out of breath through hurrying.

"They told me it was you, Bill," he pants. "What's the meaning of this?"

"Oh, the old story," replies the man. "No graft, and the missus and kids without a bite. I spotted the baker's barrer and the temptation was too much, knowin' as 'ow they wos 'ungry."

"Umph!" said the policeman, fumbling in his trousers pocket. "I'm a married man myself, and I know. Here, missus, take this and get a bit o' grub and some coal while I see if something can't be done for you. Come on, Bill, it's got to be got over; they won't be hard on you, it's your first offence."

Food and warmth and some degree of cheerfulness walk into that house, not because the policeman walked out, but because he walked in!

Next day, at the police-court, Constable X says:

"From information received, I went to the prisoner's home; his wife and children were eating greedily at parts of the loaf. Prisoner admitted he had stolen it as his family was starving. Prisoner didn't eat any himself. There was no fire, y'r worship, and no milk for the baby, so I —" —here the officer stammers and blushes a rosy red. "Honest, respectable man, but out o' work," adds the officer.

"Very praiseworthy indeed," remarks the magistrate, knowing full well what had happened from past experience.

"I want my mummy! I want my mummy!" sobs a dirty-faced little urchin in the street.

What's the matter, my little woman— lost yourself?"

"Y-y-y-e-e-s," wails the lost one.

"Where d'ye live?" queries the fatherly constable.

"B-d-d-dunno!" is the reply.

"Well, you come along o' uncle, and we'll soon find mother," is the comforting answer; and often, if the little mite is too tired to walk, a burly policeman will pick her up in his arms and walk through the streets to the station with his find.

"Pore little dear; lorst, she is," remark sympathetic mothers as the little procession of lost child, grimy-faced urchins and constable make their way to the station.

Once inside, a rug in front of the fire, cakes and milk —all provided by "uncle" who found the little stray —and the telephone wires at work to all stations in the neighbourhood. Soon, very soon, an anxious mother, living perhaps a mile or so away, learns that the mite she has missed is safe in the hands of the police.

"What's the matter, chum?" says a man in uniform to a down-and-out specimen of humanity huddled in a doorway.

"Only the usual," hopelessly replies the outcast. "Demobbed and find my job filled."

"Hungry?"

"Hungry! Ain't had a square meal since I left the old 27th."

"In the old 27th, were you. Under old Garside?"

"Yus. With 'im at Loos."

"So was I. Here, get yourself a bite and a cup at the coffee-stall, and you come down to the police-court in the mornin' and I'll speak to our missionary chap. Maybe he can help you."

"I am afraid you must pay a fine. I'll make it a light one, but you must not keep a dog without a licence," said the magistrate to an old woman.

"It was my boy's, and he was killed in the war," sobbed the defendant.

Half an hour after the old woman left the court smiling. Her fine was paid and she had a brand-new licence in her hand. Some of the constables at the back of the court had clubbed together, paid the fine, and taken out a licence for the old woman.

A policeman is one of the most human men in the world, because he sees so much trouble.

Stolen — One Row of Houses!

Only once is it recorded that a row of houses was stolen. How, is described below.

TO steal a house may seem a feat almost impossible of accomplishment; more like a fairy-tale than fact.

Nevertheless, it has been done, though only a few times during the years records have been kept of London's criminal history. Stealing a row of them is even rarer.

It is not like stealing a suit-case, but it is, after all, quite easy, provided the owner of the property is not on hand to cry "Stop thief!"

All that is required is unbounded confidence and luck. Add to this an air of responsibility and the knowledge of the address of some house-demolisher of good repute—and there you are!

In all criminal enterprises there is an element of gambling. And it is a question well worthy of consideration by Scotland Yard whether the excitement of the gamble —your personal liberty plus some gain against a spell in prison —does not form one of the strongest elements of the average criminal's existence.

Less than twenty years ago there were three empty houses standing in a terrace of ten. The terrace itself stood in what was then a very good class residential district off Tottenham Court Road.

A house-agent's board for five or more years had indicated that these house's were "To Let," but in spite of bills in the window indicating that they were "very desirable," and that the rent was "moderate," no one seemed to take enough interest in them even to the extent of wishing to look them over.

Slowly at first, and then more rapidly as time went on, signs of decay made themselves apparent.

Windows were broken; bell-pulls hung limp; the door-knockers disappeared, and stray cats came on the scene and took possession.

Finally, even the house-agents lost interest, for people eventually forgot to whom the houses belonged.

Then, one fine day in May, 19—, a gang of men appeared on the scene and ran up a hoarding round the houses, putting up a board which told all and sundry that Messrs. X, House Demolisher, —— Street, N.W., would give estimates free for pulling down old houses.

In due course windows and doors were taken out, chimney-pots were tumbled from their dizzy heights.

All this did not pass unnoticed, and a constable on the beat observed these happenings and copied down the address of the contractor in his pocket-book and reported the affair at Tottenham Court Road Police Station at the end of his tour of duty.

Official inquires showed that Messrs. X was a well-established contractor, a man of unblemished character, and not one who would be likely to lend himself to underhand proceedings.

When questioned, he said that his instructions came from the owner, and as nobody knew who the owner was and could query the name, the inquiry ended.

Finally, the last load of bricks and rubbish had been carted away, and nothing remained of the houses once behind the hoarding but a heap of valueless debris.

Less than a month later, a well-dressed man, bronzed by travel, came to a halt in — Street outside the hoarding where the houses had stood.

Five minutes afterwards the same man stood in Tottenham Court Road Police Station, complaining that someone had "stolen his houses."

He had been away in South America, and had almost forgotten about them.

It took some time to convince the police officials that such a thing as stealing a row of houses had actually occurred, and that under their very noses.

Patient inquiry revealed that the police actually had a record of the theft, though not under that heading. The "Occurrence Book" showed that in the previous month a report had been made by the constable on that beat of the demolition of these particular houses by Messrs. X.

X was seen, and admitted having pulled down these houses, and stated in addition that he had paid fifty pounds to a man who represented he was the owner for the privilege of doing so. He said that he would know the man again.

His address was given to the police, and, of course, proved to be false.

Just as all hope of tracing the house-stealer had been abandoned, Mr. X was standing by another job in South London when he happened to see the man for whom the police and the real owner of Nos. 8, 9, and 10, — Street were looking.

He detained him in conversation until a constable came in sight, and then he gave him into custody. The house-thief was sent to penal servitude for five years, thus proving that house-stealing, even when the owner is away, has its risks.

The Last Days of Jim the Penman

By Herbert Asbury.

Jim the Penman, the Wizard of the Quill, was one of the most famous criminals of modern times. Yet, while his extraordinary achievements have been told in many tongues, few people know who he really was. His early history, together with some of his more famous exploits, are recorded in the following authentic article.

Just as the detective reached the roof, Jim the Penman emerged from a chute and faced him with a loaded revolver in each hand.

JIM THE PENMAN was one of the most expert forgers and confidence men who ever operated anywhere in the world.

He made hundreds of thousands of pounds by his remarkable facility with the pen; he led the gullible through the tricks and devices of the "con men," and garnered other thousands from them by the most extraordinary and ingenious schemes.

But in the end he went straight down the trail that all of the great criminals have travelled; and the end of Jim the Penman came only a few months ago, when he stood before the authorities of Livingston

County, New York, and humbly asked admittance to the poorhouse.

The famous forger, old and penniless and broken in health, is now a county charge— and in the town where he was born.

The real name of Jim the Penman is Alonzo J. Whiteman, and his career probably never has been equalled in the criminal world.

The wildest imaginings never have been more remarkable than the true story of Whiteman's life.

Born and brought up in the lap of luxury, literally with a silver spoon in his month, he was the possessor of a clean, honestly made fortune before he was thirty years old.

He was a candidate for mayor of a great American city, a leader in the business and social life of his adopted city —and now, at the age of sixty-one, an inmate of an almshouse, dependent for his livelihood upon a government whose laws he has broken, and a people whose money he has stolen.

A Clean Start.

In the early part of his career, Whiteman was neither a forger nor a confidence man, although, even when he was a boy, he had a notable gift of penmanship.

In his early youth, Whiteman was no more a criminal than any other boy of his age,

His one besetting sin was gambling, and it was this, a constitutional inability to stay out of a game of poker or resist the click of the dice, that even an outcast, hunted down by the detectives and the police of a hundred cities.

At the height of his career, someone asked a well-known detective agency for a brief report on Whiteman, and this was what the agency sent out:

"Arrested forty-seven times. Convicted and served time twice. Called 'Jim the Penman' and 'King of Forgers.'"

Brief, but expressive.

Whiteman's family for several generations has been one of the prominent families of Livingston County, New York, and it was there, in the little town of Dansville, that Jim the Penman was born.

His parents were wealthy, and young Whiteman grew through boyhood to manhood, surrounded by everything that could possibly make for right and clean living, and everything that money could buy.

He went to Hamilton College when he was approaching his twenties, and from there, after graduating with an A.B., he went to

Columbia University in New York City, where he received a law degree.

When Whitman came out of Columbia, his father decided to send him West to handle some of the Whiteman properties in that section of the country, and the boy set out for Duluth.

Even at that time he was wild and addicted to the gaming-tables, but his parents believed that it was merely the natural exuberance and wildness of youth, and they thought he would settle down when he saw real work ahead of him.

And a Busy One.

He reached Duluth, and plunged with characteristic energy and enthusiasm into his father's business.

For a long time he seemed to have lived a quiet and useful life, devoting himself to work, and so well did he handle his father's interests that the elder Whiteman made him a gift of ten thousand pounds, probably the first really large sum that the boy had ever had.

This was followed on his twenty-fifth birthday by another gift of twenty-five thousand pounds.

And only a few years later the elder Whiteman died, and the man who later became known the length and breadth of the land as Jim the Penman and King of Forgers received about £250,000 as his share of the Whiteman fortune.

Young Whiteman had not been in Duluth more than a few months before he became interested in politics.

His ability won him a place in the State assembly, and when he was only twenty-six, he was elected to the State senate, the youngest man ever to hold such an office in Minnesota.

Altogether, he was in the Minnesota legislature for four years, and appears to have made a creditable record.

He left the senate to run for Congress, the equivalent of our Parliament, but was defeated; and later he was defeated for mayor of Duluth, although he made a strong showing, and lost out by a very narrow margin.

He retrieved his political fortunes somewhat by being elected to head the Minnesota delegation to the national Democratic convention, which nominated Grover Cleveland for President. He always claimed that it was his influence and hard work which obtained the nomination for the candidate.

It may not be that this claim is true, but it is certain that for many years Whiteman was a power in Minnesota and North-West politics, and that he became a campaign orator of considerable prominence and not a little ability.

Bankrupt.

The turning-point in Whiteman's life, the thing that eventually made him a criminal, hounded from coast to coast, came about at this time, when his political fortunes were at their height, and when close application would have sent him to enviable heights.

He began speculating in Wall Street, and shortly after he received his inheritance he was one of the thousands who were squeezed unmercifully in the collapse of the Leiter wheat corner.

He lost a fair share of his fortune there, and, in vain efforts to get his money back, during the next two years he lost everything he had.

In 1897, nine years after he had inherited more than a quarter of a million sterling, he was penniless.

He went to work in a Duluth bank for small pay, and held the place for some time; but his years of wealth had unfitted him for such a minor role, and he went to New York, hoping that he might do better there.

New York proved too large a city for him. He was unable to resist the temptations of the metropolis.

He had not been there more than a few months when he fell in with criminals, principally forgers and confidence men, and that was the beginning of the end, so far as decent citizenship was concerned.

From that time forward his history is a succession of crimes and narrow escapes from being imprisoned.

He was ever after a criminal, until the day finally came when he stood before the authorities in his home town and asked that he be allowed to spend the remainder of his life in the poorhouse.

Whiteman came to be a consummate operator, committing crimes of the most intricate and subtle character.

A Tricky Customer.

When he ran foul of the police —and that was often —he manifested such knowledge of the law and of human nature that he was able to use the detectives themselves to help him out of the net they spread for him.

The fact that he was arrested forty-seven times and convicted only twice, proved his skill and cleverness.

He was not afraid to take a chance, and he did not take desperate chances; he applied to his forgings and his confidence work an ability and an intelligence that in other lines probably would have recouped his fortune and earned him the lasting respect of his fellow-citizens.

At the time when Whiteman was known as Jim the Penman and King of Forgers, and when the police from New York to California were laying schemes to trap him, he was the head and the directing brain of a gang of forgers whose operations probably never have been equalled in the United States.

This group included such noted criminals as Knox, Witherout, Warren, Boothman, Wickwire, and Gordon, and in ten years they amassed a sum, through their illegal operations, which has been estimated variously at from £100,000 to £500,000.

They used various devices, all dominated by forgery and fraud. Their victims usually were hotels and banks, although, as a rule, the hotels contributed little more than the living of the gang, while their big hauls were made from the banks.

Knox, who was the right-hand man of Jim the Penman, was the son of a clergyman in Elmira, New York, and a class-mate of Whiteman's at Hamilton College.

He was a lawyer and an excellent penman.

The Partnership.

Knox and Whiteman had been boys together, but when Whiteman went to Duluth, Knox remained in Elmira.

He heard of his friend's success in Duluth, and he went at once to the Western city.

At that time both of them were straight enough, but they loved to gamble, and they wanted to win; they did not care how they won.

They joined forces to beat the poker game at the Duluth City Club, and they did it so successfully that a scandal arose which compelled Knox to leave the city.

It was then arranged that Knox should go to Mexico, and establish a credit for the purchase of diamonds, to be paid for with cheques on the bank in Duluth with which Whiteman did business.

The scheme was to pay the cheques until the confidence of the Mexican dealers had been obtained, and then Knox was to make a big purchase, present bogus cheques in payment, and hasten across the boundary line into the United States with the booty.

But Whiteman became careless, and allowed one of the early cheques to go to be queried, and Knox was arrested when he tried to swing the big deal.

He spent two years in a Mexican prison.

Not long afterward, Whiteman, after collapsing financially, went to New York, and soon began the organisation of the gang of forgers, which was joined by Knox when he was released from the Mexican gaol.

The gang chose Pawtucket, Rhode Island, as the scene of its first operation, and, going to that town, Jim the Penman bought a cotton-mill for £12,000.

They deposited a draft in the usual manner, and immediately drew out one thousand pounds against it.

With this cash they went to Pittsburg and opened an account in a bank there, also making a deposit in a bank at McKeesport, Pennsylvania.

Then they began drawing from one into the other in order to swell the volume of their transaction at each bank, and make it appear that they dealt in big sums.

Bowled Out.

But unfortunately for them, the McKeesport bank was the correspondent of the Pittsburgh bank, and the officials made mutual inquiries, with the result that when the gang tried to draw out a considerable sum, their arrest was ordered.

All of them escaped, however, and went to Canada, where one of them introduced himself as Thomas W. Lawson, the Boston financier, and negotiated for the purchase of a copper mine at a purchase price of £250,000. With this as a basis, the gang sold sight drafts on a Boston bank for £500, and with this money they returned to New York.

But the police were waiting for them, and every member of the gang was arrested.

One was convicted for the cotton-mill job. Knox was sent to Pittsburg, convicted and sentenced to an indeterminate sentence in the State's prison.

Whiteman was sent to New York, but the police did not have sufficient evidence to hold him, and Jim the Penman was released.

Not long afterwards, Knox became (*unreadable*) . . . board of pardons and parole, and Whiteman went to Harrisburg, posed as a member of the New York State legislature, and pleaded Knox's case so successfully that the (*unreadable*) . . . to return to New York with

Whiteman.

Once, in the metropolis they immediately became involved in forgeries against the Nassau Trust Company and other Trust companies in New York and Brooklyn.

Jim the Penman was arrested when, in the company of a young woman, he was about to board a tramcar in the city of St. Louis.

The Last Crime.

The particular crime for which Whiteman finally went to prison for a long term was committed in 1904.

In July of that year, a messenger; appeared at the Fidelity Trust

Company in Buffalo, with a letter typewritten on what purported (*unreadable*) . . . East Aurora concern, and signed F. H. Hubbard, who appeared to be a member of the firm.

Enclosed in the letter was a draft for £2,000 to Hubbard's order by the cashier of the National Hudson River Bank of Hudson, New York, and on the Leather Manufacturers' Bank of New York City.

"I wish to open an account," the letter said. "I am an invalid and seldom leave East Aurora. Please send me by return messenger a cheque book."

The bank accepted the draft, and the £2,000 was credited to Hubbard. Then, after allowing sufficient time for the draft to pass through the usual channels, the Trust Company permitted Hubbard to draw on the account.

Whiteman and Joseph Boothman, who was associated with him in this enterprise, succeeded in drawing out almost a thousand pounds before the banks realised that a swindle had been perpetrated.

At that time the Pinkertons were under contract with the American Bankers' Association to protect the member banks against forgeries, and they immediately arrested Boothman, but Whiteman escaped.

He was arrested as he was about to board a Delmar Avenue car in St. Louis with a young woman.

The Escape.

Whiteman said he knew nothing of the Buffalo crime, but he agreed to return to Buffalo without waiting for extradition proceedings.

Detective Al Solomon of the Buffalo Police Department, and Detective Fields of the Pinkertons, were assigned to take him back East, and they anticipated no trouble.

Nothing happened until they reaches Dunkirk, only about fifty miles from Buffalo.

There the train stopped, and the two detectives and their prisoner got off and walked up and down the station platform to warm themselves up a bit.

When the train was about to start, one of the detectives climbed aboard, then Whiteman, and then the other detective.

As they reached the doorway of the stateroom, which they had occupied during the long ride from St. Louis, Whiteman suddenly turned and pointed out of a window.

"Look!" he cried. "What's that?"

The two detectives turned involuntarily, and Whiteman quickly stepped inside the stateroom and slammed the door as the detectives threw their weight against it.

Then the train started, and when the detectives finally opened the door, they found that Whiteman had jumped out of the window and was gone.

The train was going fifty miles an hour by that time; it reached the next station in twenty minutes. The detectives hurried back to Dunkirk, but they found no sign of Whiteman.

The forger said later that after he had dropped from the window of the train he simply mingled with the crowd about the station for a few minutes and then went to the Erie Hotel and registered.

He went to bed and slept soundly until the next morning, and when he came downstairs, he was surprised to find that the two detectives had occupied a room on the same floor.

He had breakfast in the hotel, white the detectives slept upstairs, and then caught the first train to Dansville, where his mother still lived.

Home Again.

Whiteman remained in hiding at his mother's home several months, while the detectives scoured the country for him.

He went to Mexico and, after staying there a few months, went back to Dansville. Once more he went away, visited the South, and returned.

It was then that the Pinkertons heard that Jim the Penman was at the home of his mother, and sent seven of their best detectives with six Buffalo detectives to capture him.

The officers came into the town in the dead of night, because they had heard that the townspeople believed in the innocence of Whiteman, and they feared trouble would ensue if they tried to take him out of the town.

They came quietly, however, and had surrounded the Whiteman home before anyone in Dansville knew of their presence, and, when it was too late to warn the forger, one of the detectives rapped on the door, which was opened by Mrs. Whiteman.

"What do you want?" she demanded.

"Is your son here?" inquired the detective.

Mrs. Whiteman slammed the door in their faces and locked it

before they could force it open.

Then somewhere in the house a buzzer sounded and aroused Whiteman, who was asleep in a room on the top floor, dressed and prepared to escape.

Finally the door opened, and Mrs. Whiteman appeared.

"My son is not here," she said. "You had better go away."

"We know he is here," said the detective. "We must search the house."

Mrs. Whiteman finally agreed to admit them if they would wait until she and the other members of the family had dressed. Finally the detectives entered.

"I have not seen my son for several months," the forger's mother said. "I do not know where he is."

"We've trailed him here," the detectives told her, "He is hidden here somewhere."

The Capture.

They searched the house, but they found no trace of the forger. They were about to leave, when one of them, tapping against the wall, discovered that it was hollow.

He quickly moved a big oil painting aside and found a secret opening which seemed to lead into a chute.

Climbing through the chute, the detectives discovered that it extended through the roof; from the outside it resembled a chimney.

They concluded that Whiteman was hiding in the chute above the house, and one of them immediately climbed up, leaving a guard inside the house.

Just as the detective reached the roof, Whiteman clambered out of the chute and stood facing two loaded and cocked revolvers.

"We've got you now, all right!" cried the detective.

"Think so?" sneeringly asked Whiteman.

He suddenly threw himself face downward on the icy roof and slid down to the eaves.

For a moment, he hung by his finger tips twenty-five feet above the ground, where half a dozen detectives stood waiting for him to drop. He fell and landed ingloriously in a snowdrift, out of which the policemen dug him.

Then they hustled him into a sleigh and drove over the county line before his people could summon their friends and neighbours and rescue him.

Jim the Penman was convicted for the Buffalo crime, and after he was released from prison in 1914, he went to work, doing odd jobs here and there, earning just enough to keep body and soul together.

His old cunning with the pen was gone for ever. Finally his health became so poor, and he became so feeble, that he was not able to work any longer.

It was then that he went to the town where he was born, and applied for admission to the county poorhouse.

TREASURE ISLAND
The Greatest Story of Pirate Gold and Pirate Adventure the World has Ever Known.
By Robert Louis Stevenson.
IF YOU'VE MISSED ANY OF IT
Get back numbers if you can, and read, this stirring story in full. A summary can't do it justice, but this will give you the gist of what has happened already.

IN the year of grace 17— there came to our inn, the Admiral Ben bow, near Bristol, a curious customer who was to bring a world of trouble (and adventure) to my widowed mother and me, Jim Hawkins.

He was a seafaring man, whom we came to call the "Captain" until we knew his real name, which was Billy Bones.

After a time one of the Captain's old cronies appeared at the inn. With him was a band of his pirate companions, and they sought something in the Captain's sea-chest— something they called "Flint's Fist."

But they did not get it because I had already taken it in part payment for lodging-money owed to my mother, the Captain being already dead of an apoplexy brought on by fright concerning the pirates.

I took my tale to good Dr. Livesey. He and the squire examined the packet I obtained —which was indeed "Flint's Fist," the chart of an island containing treasure buried by the notorious buccaneer, Captain Flint, and given by him at his death to our lodger, Billy Bones, who was his first mate.

Squire Trelawney said he would fit up an expedition to go in search of this treasure, starting from Bristol in three weeks' time. The doctor also, and me —Jim Hawkins —to be cabin-boy.

In due course a ship was bought and fitted —the Hispaniola. The squire, who had been making all arrangements, wrote to say he had found a than named Long John Silver, whom he engaged as ship's cook, and who in turn recommended him to many likely-looking tough old salts for the voyage.

And then I journeyed down to Bristol, ready for my great adventure.

The squire gave me a note to John Silver, at his inn by the waterside at the sign of the Spy-Glass.

I introduced myself, and hardly had we exchanged a word or two when a man got up from one of the benches and made off furtively. It was Black Dog, one of the men who had visited the Captain at the Admiral Benbow.

I raised the alarm, but everybody denied knowledge of him, and though he was pursued, he was not caught. Long John Silver and I then went back to the inn, where the doctor and the squire were staying, and told of the occurrence.

The squire gave Long John instructions to have all hands aboard the Hispaniola by four that afternoon, and the squire, the doctor, and I went aboard at once.

When we arrived, Captain Smollett sought out the squire. He had a grievance. He had been engaged to sail under sealed orders, but every man before the mast knew more than he did. The hands knew that they were after treasure, and somebody had blabbed.

"It's my belief," he said, "that neither of you gentlemen know what you're about; but I'll tell you my way of it —life or death, and a close run!"

(Now go ahead with this week's gripping instalment.)

Powder and Arms, (Continued).

"THAT is all clear, and, I dare say, true enough," replied Dr. Livesey. "We take the risk, but we are not so ignorant as you believe us. Next, you say you don't like the crew. Are they not good seamen?"

"I don't like them, sir," returned Captain Smollett. "And I think I should have had the choosing of my own hands, if you go to that."

"Perhaps you should," replied the doctor. "My friend should, perhaps, have taken you along with him; but the slight, if there be one, was unintentional. And you don't like Mr. Arrow?"

"I don't, sir. I believe he's a good seaman; but he's too free with the crew to be a good officer."

"Well, now, and the short and the long of it, captain?" asked the doctor. "Tell us what you want."

"Well, gentlemen, are you determined to go on this cruise?"

"Like iron," answered the squire.

"Very good," said the captain. "Then, as you've heard me very patiently, saying things that I could not prove, hear me a few words more. They are putting the powder and the arms in the fore hold. Now, you have a good place under the cabin; why not put them there —first-point. Then you are bringing four of your own people with you, and they tell me some of them are to be berthed forward. Why not give them the berths here beside the cabin? —second point."

"Any more?" asked Mr. Trelawney.

"One more," said the captain. "There's been too much blabbing already."

"Far too much," agreed the doctor.

"I'll tell you what I've heard myself," continued Captain Smollett, "That you have a map of an island; that there's crosses on the map to show where treasure is; and that the island lies —"

And then he named the latitude and longitude exactly.

"I never told that," cried the squire, "to a soul!"

"The hands know it, sir," returned the captain.

"Livesey, that must have been you or Hawkins," cried the squire.

"It doesn't much matter who it was," replied the doctor; and I could see that neither he nor the captain paid much regard to Mr. Trelawney's protestations. Neither did I, to be sure; he was so loose a talker. Yet in this case I believe he was really right, and that nobody had told the situation of the island.

"Well, gentlemen," continued the captain, "I don't know who has this map; but I make it a point, it shall be kept secret even from me and Mr. Arrow. Otherwise I would ask you to let me resign."

"I see," Said the doctor. "You wish us to keep this matter dark, and to make a garrison of the stern part of the ship, manned with my friend's own people, and provided with all the arms and powder on board. In other words, you fear a mutiny."

"Sir," said Captain Smollett, "with no intention to take offence, I deny your right to put words into my mouth. No captain, sir, would be justified in going to sea at all if he had ground enough to say that. As for Mr. Arrow, I believe him thoroughly honest; some of the men are same; all may be for all I know. But I am responsible for the ship's safety and the life of every man Jack aboard of her. I see things going, as I think, not quite right, and I ask you to take certain precautions, or let me resign my berth. And that's all."

"Captain Smollett," began the doctor, with a smile, "did ever you hear the fable of the mountain and the mouse? You'll excuse me, I dare say, but you remind me of that fable. When you came in here I'll stake my wig you meant more than this."

"Doctor," said the captain, "you are smart. When I came in here I meant to get discharged. I had no thought that Mr. Trelawney would hear a word."

"No more I would," cried the squire. "Had Livesey not been here I should have seen you to the deuce. As it is, I have heard you. I will do as you desire; but I think the worse of you."

"That's as you please, sir," said the captain. "You'll find I do my duty." And with that he took his leave.

"Trelawney," said the doctor, "contrary to all my notions, I believe you have managed to get two honest men on board with you —that man and John Silver."

"Silver, if you like," cried the squire; "but as for that intolerable humbug, I declare I think his conduct unmanly, un-sailorly, and downright un-English."

"Well," says the doctor, "we shall see."

When we came on deck, the men had begun to take out the arms and powder, yo-ho-ing at their work, while the captain and Mr. Arrow stood by superintending.

The new arrangement was quite to my liking. The whole schooner had been overhauled; six berths had been made astern, out of what had been the after-part of the main hold; and this set of cabins was only joined to the galley and forecastle by a sparred passage on the port side. It had been originally meant that the captain, Mr. Arrow, Hunger, Joyce, the doctor, and the squire, were to occupy these six berths. Now, Redruth and I were to get two of them, and Mr. Arrow and the captain were to sleep on deck in the companion, which had been enlarged on each side till you might almost have called it a round-house. Very low it was still, of course; but there was room to swing two hammocks, and even the mate seemed pleased with the arrangement. Even he, perhaps, had been doubtful as to the crew, but that is only guess, for, as you shall hear, we had not long the benefit of his opinion.

We were all hard at work, changing the powder and the berths, when the last man or two, and Long John along with them, came off in a shore-boat.

The cook came up the side like a monkey for cleverness, and, as soon as he saw what was doing, "So ho, mates!" says he, "what's this?"

"We're a-changing of the powder, Jack," answers one,

"Why, by the powers," cried Long John, "if we do, we'll miss the morning tide!"

"My orders!" said the captain shortly. "You may go below, my man. Hands will want supper."

"Ay, ay, sir," answered the cook; and, touching his forelock, he disappeared at once in the direction of his galley.

"That's a good man, captain," said the doctor.

"Very likely, sir," replied Captain Smollett. "Easy with that, men —easy," he ran on, to the fellows who were shifting the powder; and then suddenly observing me examining the swivel we carried amidships, a long brass nine. "Here, you ship's boy," he cried, "out of that! Off with you to the cook and get some work."

And then as I was hurrying off I heard him say, quite loudly, to the doctor:

"I'll have no favourites on my ship."

I assure you I was quite of the squire's way of thinking, and hated the captain deeply.

The Voyage.

ALL that night we were in a great bustle getting things stowed in their place, and boatfuls of the squire's friends, Mr. Blandly and the like, coming off to wish him a good voyage and a safe return. We never had a night at the Admiral Benbow when I had half the work; and I was dog-tired when, a little before dawn, the boatswain, sounded his pipe, and the crew began to man the capstan-bars. I might have been twice as weary, yet I would not have left the deck; all was so new and interesting to me —the brief commands, the shrill note of the whistle, the men bustling to their places in the glimmer of the ship's lanterns.

"Now, Barbecue, tip us a stave," cried one voice.

"The old one," cried another.

"Ay, ay, mates," said Long John, who was standing by with his crutch under his arm and at once broke out in the air and words I knew so well:

"Fifteen men on The Dead Man's Chest—

And then the whole crew bore chorus:

"Yo-ho-ho, and a bottle of rum!"

And at the third "ho!" drove the bars before them with a will.

Even at that exciting moment it carried me back to the old Admiral Benbow in a second; and I seemed to hear the voice of the captain piping in the chorus. But soon the anchor was short up; soon it was hanging dripping at the bows; soon the sails began to draw, and the land and shipping to flit by on either side; and before I could lie down to snatch an hour of slumber the Hispaniola had begun her voyage to the Isle of Treasure.

I am not going to relate that voyage in detail. It was fairly prosperous. The ship proved to be a good ship, the crew were capable seamen, and the captain thoroughly understood his business. But before we came the length of Treasure Island, two or three things had happened which require to be known.

Mr. Arrow, first of all, turned out even worse than the captain had feared. He had no command among the men, and people did what they pleased with him. But that was by no means the worst of it; for after a day or two at sea he began to appear on deck with hazy eye, red cheeks, stuttering tongue, and other marks of drunkenness. Time after time he was ordered below in disgrace. Sometimes he fell and cut himself; sometimes he lay all day long in his little bunk at one side of the companion; sometimes for a day or two he would be almost sober and attend to his work at least passably.

In the meantime we could never make out where he got the drink. That was the ship's mystery. Watch him as we pleased, we could do nothing to solve it; and when we asked him to his face, he would only laugh, if he were drunk, and if he were sober, deny solemnly that he ever tasted anything but water.

He was not only useless as an officer and a bad influence amongst the men, but it was plain that at this rate he must soon kill himself outright; so nobody was much surprised, nor very sorry, when one dark night, with a head sea, he disappeared entirely and was seen no more.

"Overboard!" said the captain. "Well, gentlemen, that saves the trouble of putting him in irons."

But there we were, without a mate; and it was necessary, of course, to advance one of the men. The boatswain, Job Anderson, was the likeliest man aboard, and, though he kept his old title, he served in a way as mate. Mr. Trelawney had followed the sea and his knowledge made him very useful, for he often took a watch himself in easy weather. And the coxswain, Israel Hands, was a careful, wily, old, experienced seaman, who could be trusted at a pinch with almost anything.

He was a great confidant of Long John Silver, and so the mention of his name leads me on to speak of our ship's cook, Barbecue, as the men called him.

Aboard ship he carried his crutch by a lanyard round his neck, to have both hands as free as possible. It was something to see him wedge the foot of the crutch against a bulkhead, and, propped against it, yielding to every movement of the ship, get on with his cooking like someone safe ashore. Still more strange was it to see him in the heaviest of weather cross the deck. He had a line or two rigged up to help him across the widest spaces—Long John's earrings, they were called; and he would hand himself from one place to another, now using the crutch, now trailing it alongside by the lanyard, as quickly as another man could walk. Yet some of the men who had sailed with him before expressed their pity to see him so reduced.

"He's no common man, Barbecue," said the coxswain to me. "He had good schooling in his young days, and can speak like a book when so minded; and brave —a lion's nothing alongside of Long John! I seen him grapple four, and knock their heads together —him unarmed!"

All the crew respected him and even obeyed him. He had a way of talking to each, and doing everybody some particular service. To me he was unweariedly kind; and always glad to see me in the galley, which he kept as clean as a new pin; the dishes hanging up burnished, and his parrot in a cage in one corner.

"Come away, Hawkins," he would say; "come and have a yarn with John. Nobody more welcome than yourself, my son. Sit you down and hear the news. Here's Cap'n Flint —I calls my parrot Cap'n Flint, after the famous buccaneer —here's Cap'n Flint predicting success to our v'vage. Wasn't you, cap'n?"

And the parrot would say, with great rapidity, "Pieces of eight!

pieces of eight! pieces of eight!" till you wondered that he was not out of breath, or till John threw his handkerchief over the cage.

"Now, that bird," he would say, "is, may be, two hundred years old, Hawkins —they lives for ever mostly; and if anybody's seen more wickedness, it must be the devil himself. She's sailed with England, the great Cap'n England, the pirate. She's been at Madagascar, and at Malabar, and Surinam, and Providence, and Portobello. She was at the fishing up of the wrecked plate ships. It's there she learned 'Pieces of eight,' and little wonder, three hundred and fifty thousand of 'em, Hawkins! She was at the boarding of the Viceroy of the Indies out of Goa, she was; and to look at her you would think she was a baby. But you smelt powder —didn't you, cap'n?"

"Stand by to go about," the parrot would scream.

"Ah, she's a handsome craft, she is," the cook would say, and give her sugar from his pocket, and then the bird would peck at the bars and swear straight on, passing belief for wickedness. "There," John would add. "you can't touch pitch and not be mucked, lad. Here's this poor old innocent bird o' mine swearing blue fir a, and none the wiser, you may lay to that. She would swear the same, in a manner of speaking, before chaplain." And John would touch his forelock with a solemn way he had, that made me think he was the best of men.

In the meantime, squire and Captain Smollett were still on pretty distant terms with one another. The squire made no bones about the matter; he despised the captain. The captain, on his part, never spoke but when he was spoken to, and then sharp and short and dry, and not a word wasted. He owned, when driven into a corner, that he seemed to have been wrong about the crew, that some of them were as brisk as he wanted to see, and all had behaved fairly well. As for the ship, he had taken a downright fancy to her,

"She'll lie a point nearer the wind than a man has a right to expect of his own married wife, sir. But," he would add, "all I say is, we're not home again, and I don't like the cruise."

The squire, at this, would turn away and march up and down the deck, chin in air.

"A trifle more of that man," he would say, "and I should explode."

We had some heavy weather, which only proved the qualities of the Hispaniola. Every man on board seemed well content, and they must have been hard to please if they had been otherwise, for it is my belief there was never a ship's company so spoiled since Noah put to sea. Double grog was going on the least excuse there was duff on odd days, as, for instance, if the squire heard it was any man's birthday.

"Never knew good come of it yet," the captain said to Dr. Livesey. "Spoil foc's'le hands, make devils. That's my belief."

But good did come of the apple barrel, as you shall hear, for if it had not been for that, we should have had no note of warning, and might all have perished by the hand of treachery.

This w as how it came about.

We had run up the trades to get the wind of the island we were after—I am not allowed to be more plain—and now we were running down for it with a bright look-out day and night. It was about the last day of our outward voyage, by the largest computation. Some time that night, or, at latest, before noon of the morrow, we should sight the Treasure Island. We were heading S.S.W., and had a steady breeze abeam and a quiet sea. The Hispaniola roiled steadily, dipping her bowsprit now and then with a whiff of spray. All was drawing alow and aloft; everyone was in the bravest spirits, because we were now so near an end of the first part of our adventure.

Now, just after sundown, when all my work was over, and I was on my way to my berth, it occurred to me that I should like an apple. I ran on deck. The watch was all forward looking out for the island. The man at the helm was watching the luff of the sail, and whistling away gently to himself; and that was the only sound, excepting the swish of the sea against the bows and around the sides of the ship.

In I got bodily into the apple-barrel, and found there was scarce an apple left; but, sitting down there in the dark, what with the sound of the waters and the rocking movement of the ship, I had either fallen asleep, or was on the point of doing so, when a heavy man sat down with rather a clash close by. The barrel shook as he leaned his shoulders against it, and I was just about to jump up when the man began to speak. It was Silver's voice, and, before I had heard a dozen words, I would not have shown myself for all the world, but lay there, trembling and listening, in the extreme of fear and curiosity; for from these dozen words I understood that the lives of all the honest men aboard depended upon me alone.

(Another instalment of this unsurpassed story next week.)

www.ingramcontent.com/pod-product-compliance
Lightning Source LLC
Chambersburg PA
CBHW031839170626
46807CB00004B/1525